DARK
PASSIONS

On Newsstands Now:

TRUE STORY
and
TRUE CONFESSIONS
Magazines

True Story and *True Confessions* are the world's largest and best-selling women's romance magazines. They offer true-to-life stories to which women can relate.

Since 1919, the iconic *True Story* has been an extraordinary publication. The magazine gets its inspiration from the hearts and minds of women, and touches on those things in life that a woman holds close to her heart, like love, loss, family and friendship.

True Confessions, a cherished classic first published in 1922, looks into women's souls and reveals their deepest secrets.

To subscribe, please visit our website:
www.TrueRenditionsLLC.com or call **(212) 922-9244**

To find the TRUES at your local store, please visit:
www.WheresMyMagazine.com

DARK PASSIONS

From the Editors
Of *True Story* And
True Confessions

Published by True Renditions, LLC

True Renditions, LLC
105 E. 34th Street, Suite 141
New York, NY 10016

ISBN: 978-1-938877-85-8

Visit us on the web at www.truerenditionsllc.com.

Contents

FORBIDDEN LUST
I Seduced My Son's Best Friend

I heard a car door slam in the driveway as I swirled a dollop of green frosting onto a cooled Christmas tree cookie.

"Mom, I'm home!" They were words that I'd savored every day of the school year when Graf was a child, yet they sounded odd coming from a man's mouth. Odd, but sweet and satisfying. I dropped the cookie onto a tray and wiped my hands on the dish towel.

The door flew open, and I flung myself into my son's arms as he dropped a duffel bag onto the kitchen floor. I eyed it suspiciously, somehow knowing it was full of dirty laundry. Then, I smiled. It was a small price to pay for my son's company.

"Graf! You made it." I planted a kiss onto his unshaven cheek, which to his credit, he didn't try to wipe off immediately. He gently pulled away.

I hadn't seen Grafton since the summer, and I had been so excited as I waited for him to get home for the holidays. I'd spent days shopping for my son and ended up buying him two pairs of jeans, and everything else that was on his Christmas list. But, I also wrapped up a black cashmere sweater which had been on sale and which I couldn't resist buying. I knew sale items were final and couldn't be returned, but I'd hoped, as every mother of a nineteen-year-old did, to instill some sense of fashion in him.

Since he'd moved to New York City to try to make a name for himself as a musician, I didn't have much influence over him anymore. But every time I remembered how hard it had been to raise him alone after my husband had died—he'd died when my son was just five—I knew that I would always be his mother, and that I would always try to lead him in the right direction. Even though his father and I were only teenagers ourselves when we had him, I thought that I'd done a pretty good job of raising him.

Graf stepped to the side, and I quickly moved across the room to slide a second sheet of butter cookies out of the oven and to put them down onto an iron cooling rack. Graf's favorites, I knew, were always frosted with brightly-colored icings. I also knew the first batch would be devoured within minutes.

I saw movement at the door, and I looked up at the friend Graf had brought home with him.

"Mom, this is Michael."

I moved closer to the door and took our guest's hand into mine.

1

"Glad to finally meet you, Michael."

I'd known that Graf was bringing him along to spend Christmas week in Massachusetts with us. All that Graft had told me about him was that Michael Lyon was about twenty-five years old, and a fellow musician. According to my son, he played the meanest rhythm guitar that Graf had ever heard. They'd hoped to land jobs together playing for some of the New York singers, maybe write some songs, and had already written a few advertising jingles for the local radio station.

Michael's grip was firm and warm. For a moment, it sent a rush of tingling heat up my arm and across my chest. The pleasant sensation startled me, and his gaze captured mine. I watched as his full, brown lips parted slightly in a way that told me he was surprised by the connection that our contact had made, too. He gazed into my eyes for a long second before letting his vision travel to my lips as his own curled into a sensuous smile. I pulled my glance from his and it landed on the two cars that stood side-by-side in our driveway beyond our kitchen door.

I turned to Graf and blinked. "You drove up in separate cars?"

Graf was already shoveling cookies into his mouth eagerly and motioning for Michael to do the same.

"My mother makes the best cookies, man. Have some."

When Michael looked at me, a question in his eyes, I motioned for him to help himself. Before he did, he nodded to me. Again, when our vision collided, an unsteady attraction plummeted from my throat to the pit of my stomach. I felt myself swallow as I watched him rim his lips with his wet tongue.

"Yes, Mrs. Marcel, we took two cars. I had to make a stop on the way before coming here. And, Graf had an audition this afternoon in the city, so we decided to take our own cars and meet up on the road. Then, I followed him the rest of the way."

I nodded at the man. He seemed more than twenty-five years old. He was also worldly, sexy, and handsome, but I tried to push those thoughts out of my mind. It was true that I hadn't had a date for several years and had all but given up on the thought of ever meeting someone like Graf's father again. No one I'd dated in the years after had Leroy died had ever risen to his standards in my mind. I'd given up trying to find someone. So, meeting up with a sexy young guy like Michael had just gotten my juices flowing again. I told myself that that was all it was.

But, it was hard to stop the tingling heat that pressed hard against the inside of my thighs, or the numbing tightness that swelled them and firmed my nipples to rock-hard peaks at the sight of him.

I was glad when Graf spoke again. "Michael you'll be in the guest room. Come on, I'll show you." Graf lifted his friend's suitcase as Michael picked up his guitar and followed him.

The guest room! That was located right next door to my bedroom. But, who would have guessed that it would have given me a splash of excitement that I shouldn't have felt. Again, I tried to push the sudden, unwanted attraction out of my mind.

"My room is downstairs off the basement, where my drums are set up," I heard Graf saying as the two rounded the corner and slipped out of sight. But, before they did, Michael turned around to eye me one more time and to give me a knowing glance. A very sexy knowing glance. That's when I knew that I was in trouble.

The boys didn't stay long, once they'd stowed their stuff in their rooms.

"We're going into town, Mom. We're going to see if we can hook up with some of the old crowd at The Warehouse." Graf pulled an old sweatshirt over his head and brushed a kiss across my cheek as he headed for the back door.

"Uh, Graf, maybe your mother would like to join us?" Michael grinned at me before looking at my son.

Graf spun around and frowned. "Huh?"

"Are you afraid she won't fit in? You told me that she was the coolest mother you knew."

Graf took the bait and bolted to my side, draping his gangling arm around my shoulder.

"She is, man. But, still—" He hesitated.

Michael just looked at me with those dark, liquid, expressive eyes. His lips curved into a small smile.

"No, thank you," I managed to say. "That place is too loud and crowded on a Friday night."

Michael tilted his head with a slight shrug. "Then, maybe you'll join us tomorrow."

His words were like silk, and I couldn't control the shivery way they made me feel. I shuddered even harder when he reached out and took my hand for the second time that evening. His fingers, with a guitar-player's calluses, stroked my palm and felt rough against my skin. Still, his touch made me shudder in awareness of his youthful sexuality. I wanted to pull my hand away from him, but my muscles wouldn't work. And then, he gave my palm one last stroke with the flesh of his thumb and smiled at me again.

"I'm very happy to meet you." He raised an eyebrow out of sight of my son, and I knew that he meant every word of what he said and more. Against my will, I returned the emotion and instinctively rubbed his palm back.

"Yeah, yeah, Michael," my son interjected. "You already told her that. Now, let's get out of here."

The two left, but the feelings I experienced suddenly did not. I wrapped my arms across my chest and forced myself to breathe. All the warning signs were there—Michael was hot, young, and sexy. He was about fifteen years younger than I, one of my son's best friends, and I knew that I had no business feeling anything for him. But, truthfully, his gaze had cut through all of that. The touch of his hand had sent shock waves through my system and told me he was just as attracted to me. I knew I had to stop this before it could start, and felt the flood of relief pour out of me when I heard Graf's car engine start up in the yard.

I would do that—I would stop this thing in its tracks. I would concentrate on Christmas, which was two days away. And, I would stop feeling like a silly teenager with the hots for a young man.

I turned back to the cookies I was decorating and finished the job, using all my strength to put Michael out of my mind.

I went to bed early that night before the boys got home. I didn't want to embarrass Graf by waiting up for them. But, I couldn't sleep. I tossed and turned, thinking about the way that boy had made me feel.

Finally, at three in the morning, about an hour after I'd heard Michael and Graf come home and settle in for the night, I padded down to the kitchen to get a glass of milk.

The room glowed with the dim light of a nightlight I'd always left burning at night, ever since Graf was a boy. Shadows fell satiny blue across the floor, yet gave me a warm feeling as the heart of the kitchen enveloped me. I sipped some milk and reached for a cookie when I heard a sound coming from behind me. I turned to see Michael standing in the doorway.

The sight of him took my breath away. Dressed only in a pair of blue sweatpants which hugged his hips well below his navel, his body drew my vision. My gaze traveled to the swell of his muscular chest and swept over his firm, sculpted shoulders. As dark as liquid chocolate and just as tempting, his skin wrapped across the sinews in his neck. My eyes rose to take in his firm, square jaw and full, fleshy lips.

And then, our gazes met, and I heard him take in a deep, ragged breath. He moved stealthily like a tiger across the room toward me.

"Mrs. Marcel," he whispered as he approached. "Did we wake you when we got home?"

I felt my lip tremble. "No, I couldn't sleep." I pulled my glance away from him. I didn't want him to think that he was the reason I couldn't sleep.

"I see," he said as he slipped onto a chair next to mine. His knee brushed against mine, and my breath caught in my throat. "And that helps?" He motioned to the glass of milk sitting on the table in front of me.

4

I blinked. "Yes, would you like some?" Anything to take my mind off his nearness, off the potent sexuality of his half-naked body. I breathed in and smelled his maleness, as I tried to tear my eyes off of him. I stood clumsily and moved toward the refrigerator.

"Don't go to any trouble—" he began.

"It's no trouble." Pouring milk was no trouble. What was trouble was sitting right there at my kitchen table.

I started to set the glass down in front of him, but he reached out to take it from my hand. Our fingers touched, and that time, I couldn't control the tremble at the contact. Michael took the glass in one hand and with his other, he touched my hand to steady it.

"Are you cold? You're shivering," he whispered. He hadn't taken his eyes away from mine.

I tried to shake my head and to wrap my robe tighter around my body at the same time. Michael watched my hand move, and a smile rose to his lips.

"You're a beautiful woman, Mrs. Marcel," he complimented me, in a passion-filled voice.

I shook my head. "What?" I hadn't expected a sensual onslaught by guy that I'd just met. I knew I was a bit out of touch, but it all seemed very fast for me. Yet, my body responded to his words, and I felt my eyelashes flutter.

"Is this awkward for you? I mean, because of your son and all?" He brushed my hand with his fingertips again.

I shook my head. "I—"

"—I believe in honesty," he interrupted. "And, the truth is, I find you very attractive. I can tell by your reaction that I'm not alone in that assessment."

"What?" I asked weakly.

He licked his lips with his tongue and I felt juices begin to stir in my lower abdomen. His smile reached his eyes and he moved in closer to me.

"Call me a sensitive musician," he whispered, "but I believe our attraction is mutual." I could smell the faint odor of toothpaste on his breath and the smoky remains of spicy cologne on his skin. I let myself breathe in the essence of his masculinity and closed my eyes.

I was startled when he reached out to touch my cheek with his fingertips, and I blinked my eyes back open.

"Michael—" I began.

"Shhh," he said. "Don't fight this, Leola. Can I call you Leola?"

My skin shivered and my thighs trembled at his nearness. He must have known that I wouldn't dispute him calling me by my first name.

"Graf told me all about you, Leola—about your life and your

work and—" He stopped to grin. "And about how 'cool' you are." He brushed his fingertips across my cheek, and I felt paralyzed and powerless to stop him. "He's a great kid, you know?"

My son hadn't told me all that much about him, however. Of course, how could Graf have known just how intimately and quickly his friend and I would connect? I, myself, could hardly believe how attracted I was to Michael. I struggled to take a breath.

He moved in closer and brushed his full lips against mine. He tasted incredible, and I almost cried out in the dimness of the night at the gentle sensuality in that brief kiss. I let my tongue lick his flavor from my mouth.

My mind shouted for me to stop, but his hypnotic gaze silenced me. We gazed into each other's eyes for several long seconds before his vision traveled to my lips again. He nodded and took my hand into his. He stood and pulled me to stand near him. As I did, my robe gaped open and the skin of my breast flashed briefly through.

Michael didn't miss the sight. He exhaled raggedly, and I noticed that he, too, was now trembling at our closeness.

"Leola, this has got to be fate. I've never felt this type of attraction to a woman so quickly before."

He pulled me into his arms and kissed me again—that time, fully and hotly. His lips crushed against mine in fierce possession as his muscular arms drew me tighter against his body.

I couldn't pull away—couldn't push him away. So, I submitted fully to his kiss. And, when he deepened it—when he thrust his hot, wet tongue into my mouth—I breathed in to accept its potent search.

I heard him moan into my ear, the deep, guttural sound speaking volumes, and I kissed him again.

His hands found my breasts and he opened my robe to explore the heat of my skin. My nipples clenched tighter as he rubbed them between his fingers. The action drew a swell of hot moisture to the essence of my being, and my knees nearly buckled beneath me.

My brain began to scream at me. This was wrong! This was Graf's friend, and I barely knew the man. I knew that letting him touch me so intimately was wrong.

But, my brain could not control what my body wanted, and my arms pulled Michael closer to me—close enough that I could feel his tight, hard arousal press against me with urgent want and need.

His lips found my breast and he suckled me with an intensity that brought a groan of longing from my throat. I had been too long without a man, too long without the feelings of desire—feelings that my son's friend was drawing so effortlessly out of me.

My groan turned into a whimper as Michael pulled my robe off of my shoulders and let it fall to the floor. In a moment, his sweats joined the garment on the floor, and the two of us were standing naked in my kitchen.

The pale light accentuated every dip and crease in Michael's muscular young body. Like an African god, he stood proud and tall in front of me. My eyes drank in every inch of him and I knew that I wanted him as much as he wanted me.

I should have stopped him, but I couldn't. When his fingers found the moist warm flesh between my legs, I cried out in passion.

"Oh, Michael, we can't. We shouldn't—" My voice was a hushed whisper.

His lips silenced me. He reached behind my thighs and lifted me into the air to straddle him. As he pressed me against the wall, he settled my body down onto him, and his thick column of flesh pierced my intimate, longing spot.

I gasped in pleasure as the folds of my flesh gathered around him—enveloping, welcoming, wanting. He let out a low, plaintive sound and I watched as his eyes rolled back into his head.

He moved me to the living room sofa—it was nearer than either of our bedrooms—and he laid me down onto it with gentleness and protectiveness. The tinsel on the Christmas tree across the room picked up the tiny shafts of light from the kitchen and sparkled as it moved in the soft air currents we created. The fleeting thought of what a merry Christmas it would now be darted through my brain until he kissed me hotly again and sent a rush of pulsing, warm liquid through my veins. The image of what we were doing seared itself into my mind.

And then, he parted my legs again with his hands and thrust himself into me once more. The pleasure was indescribable.

I'd never known such physical passion as Michael was heaping onto me—and into me. I wrapped my legs around his waist and willed him to continue making such intimate love to me. My body begged, and Michael delivered. So many years alone had made the waiting worthwhile. My whole being shimmered with ecstasy as Michael continued to press into me with a full and wanting desire.

He plunged deeper and deeper and brought me to the hovering edge of climactic abyss. Suddenly, we both sensed another presence in the room—a sudden, dangerous sound that was almost indiscernible had startled us both.

Michael stopped and looked over his shoulder. I looked in the same direction from where I sensed the sound had come. My eyes focused in the darkness, and I gasped.

Graf stood in the doorway, the dim light of the kitchen nightlight glowing softly from behind made him. He'd appeared like a ghost, floating at the edge of the room.

"What in the hell is going on here?" His voice was low and deep, as if he didn't want to voice out loud the shock that he must have felt.

"Graf!" I gasped.

"Mom?" Then horror took over the words. "Mom!" He must have thought Michael had picked up someone in the bar and brought her home with him, since he couldn't have seen my face from his vantage point.

"I—I can explain, honey," I told him.

My son took a step into the room to assure himself that he was seeing right. His eyes grew round and wide, and his jaw dropped. Graf struggled to take a breath. Then he just shook his head and lifted his palms to face Michael and me.

"Explain?" His voice was a raspy whisper—still questioning if what he'd seen was true. And then, his words exploded with fury. "You can explain?"

His piercing shout broke the silence of the night and frightened me. Graf had never raised his voice to me before. Never.

"Graf—" I faltered.

"You and Michael? You tramp! You just met him. How could you—in my father's house like this!" He turned on his heel and ran out of the room. I heard his footsteps pounding down the cellar stairs.

"Wait!" I called out after him, but he either hadn't heard me, or he'd just ignored it.

I gathered my robe up from the kitchen floor and glanced over to Michael, who was pulling on his sweatpants.

"Maybe I should talk to him," he said as he touched my shoulder.

"Talk to him?" I spun around to stare at the young man. The young man who, moments before, had been doing such thrilling, sexual things to my body. "Talk to him?"

"He might listen to me." Michael shrugged, and we both knew that Graf would never listen to either of us just then.

"I can't believe I let this happen between us," I whispered.

He frowned. "It was good, Leola. You were fantastic."

I didn't want to hear that. I wanted to hear my son tell me that what I had done wasn't so bad. That he understood why his friend and I had made love.

I squeezed my eyes shut. It was impossible. He would never understand. I didn't even understand what had happened myself.

I pulled my bathrobe tighter around my naked body and shivered. I felt a tears sting the back of my eyelids, but I didn't have the time to stand wallowing in self-pity. In the background, I heard a car engine—Graf's car engine. I ran to the door, knowing my son was leaving town, was leaving our home in anger.

I couldn't let him go, so I ran out into the night and bolted into the driveway.

"Graf! Wait!" I called.

He slowed long enough to peer at me through half-narrowed eyes. The look spoke volumes of his feelings at that moment. His glance told me that he believed that his mother was a slut—a wanton woman who would sleep with a man half her age at the drop of a hat.

His look was right. The knowledge hit me right in the pit of my stomach. I didn't even know his friend, and yet, I'd had sex with him just hours after we'd met.

I swallowed hard as Graf floored his engine and spun out of the driveway.

"But, what about Christmas?" I called out after him. "What about Christmas?" I whispered into the frosty air as I saw my son's car disappearing into the night.

In another moment, Michael was standing behind me, fully dressed, his suitcase and guitar in hand.

"What are you doing?" I asked.

"I'll go after him," he said. "And, when I find him, I'll explain. I hope that I can convince him to come back here for the holiday."

I didn't understand what he was saying. I felt a if I'd ruined everything.

I padded back into the house after Michael drove away and sat down at the kitchen table. My mind flitted to the memory of him sitting there beside me before he'd taken me into the living room to make love to me.

Then, I shook it off. My indiscretion had cost me my son's respect! The panicky thought crossed my mind: What if I never saw my son again?

I sat at the kitchen table for hours. The sun came up outside, but the temperature hovered around freezing. It felt as if my heart was hovering around the freezing point, too. It was Christmas Eve, but I feared that Christmas wouldn't be coming for me that year. I'd messed up royally.

I walked over to the telephone and dialed Graf"s phone number. The machine picked up, and I silently hung up. I didn't know what to say to my son. I hoped that once I heard his voice, words of explanation would come to me. Still, I dialed again. That time, I left a message.

"Graf. I'm sorry," I said. "Can we please talk about this? Can you please come home for Christmas?"

Graf never called back. Christmas morning came and went, and my son's gifts remained unopened beneath the tree. I'd never felt so alone and empty in my life. I spent the day pacing slowly around the house, not knowing what to do or to think.

Every so often, Michael's face popped into my brain, but I pushed it aside. I tried to imagine my son's horror when he'd walked in on the two of us making love on my living room couch. I realized that I didn't think that I would be able to forgive me either, if I had been in Graf's shoes.

I walked into the kitchen and opened the refrigerator door. The Christmas ham was still in its wrapper on the top shelf, and I realized that I hadn't eaten a thing that day. I shut the door and moved to the table to the plate of cookies that Graf hadn't managed to polish off during his brief visit.

I picked up a cookie and took a bite, settling down into the chair to nibble on the rest of the treat. I hardly tasted it. My stomach still churned with the realization of what I'd done and how it had affected my son.

I picked up a reindeer cookie but tossed it back onto the plate before setting my face into my hands and weeping. Some lousy Christmas, and there was no one to blame but myself.

Suddenly, though, I heard the roar of a car engine in the yard, and I stood to get a look through the window. It was Graf's car! I ran through the door to greet him. Could it be? Was it really him?

His face was sullen and pained in a way that I'd never seen before. My heart twisted in my chest to realize I had planted that expression on my boy's sweet face. I tried to swallow the lump in my throat.

"Graf—" I began.

He brushed by me and into the house.

"Michael convinced me that I should come and talk things out with you," he said coldly.

I closed the door behind us and stood still in the corner. I wasn't sure what to say to him. I didn't want to say the wrong thing.

"He did?" I asked.

Graf turned to me with narrowed eyes. "He takes full responsibility, Mom. He says he forced himself on you." Graf rimmed his lips with his tongue. He frowned deeper. "Did he rape you, Mom?"

My mouth hung down, and I shook my head. "No, Graf. It wasn't like that. Did he tell you that?"

He breathed in deeply, and I could tell that he wanted to believe that horrible truth. I knew that he wanted me to be blameless and pure, like he believed mothers should be. But, I couldn't let him believe a lie.

"He didn't say anything, really, but he let me believe that it was something like that," he continued.

I looked at my son's pleading eyes. It would have been so easy for me to let him believe that Michael was to blame for the whole episode. If I did, I could have my son back. I could have his trust and love back in a moment.

But, I couldn't do that. It wasn't right, and it wasn't the truth. I shook my head.

10

"No, Graf. It was just something that happened between two adults. I can't really explain it."

My son's shoulders slumped. "Things like that don't just happen so fast, Mom. Nice people—good women—don't let things like that happen within hours of meeting a guy. Especially a guy who's half your age."

Now, my shoulders slumped. All the years—all the lessons I'd tried to teach my son—had been dashed by a single, brief moment in time. Yet, I still had to try to explain.

"Graf, what happened between Michael and me was something special. That kind of thing doesn't happen all the time. I don't know what came over us, but, it wasn't just sex. At least, it wasn't for me."

"Oh, yeah, right! That's what Michael said, too," he told me.

"He did?" I couldn't believe it.

Graf looked up at me with confusion in his eyes. I could tell that he was trying to see the whole thing through an adult's eyes, and I loved him even more for his confusion.

"Michael told me that he never felt that way about a woman before. I thought he was just yanking my chain," he admitted.

I rubbed my eyes and pulled at the back of my neck.

"Graf, this wasn't something planned—you know that. Maybe it shouldn't have happened, but we can't take it back now."

Graf shook his head. I knew that he was struggling with his emotions. He drew in a deep breath.

"I just don't understand it, Mom. How could you let something like that happen? With my friend, especially? He's my friend, Mom."

I let a long breath out. I didn't know what else to say to him. I looked deeply into his eyes and saw the hurtful confusion there. My heart twisted in my chest.

"Graf, it won't happen again. I promise you that," I vowed.

He slowly shook his head. Then, he frowned again. "The thing is, Mom, I've known Michael for awhile now. I've seen him go through women left and right. None of them has ever meant anything to him."

The words hit me deep in the pit of my stomach. I should have known that my son's friend was only out to get whatever he could from a desperate, older woman. Shame filtered over me.

"But, Mom, this time, I think it was different. I know it was different," he admitted.

My eyes darted to Graf's face. "What?"

"He was really upset about the whole thing. I've never seen him like that before." Graf scratched his head. "I think he really likes you, Mom." He padded across the floor and sat down on a kitchen chair. "Is that possible?"

"Possible for him to like me?" I repeated.

11

"No, I mean—of course, it's possible. But, is there really such a thing as love at first sight?" He drew in a deep breath. "Because that's what he said. He said he thinks he fell in love with you the moment he saw you."

"Michael said that?" The words were magic to my ears.

"He said it's never happened to him before," he confessed.

"He said that?" I sank into a chair beside my son.

"And, I meant it, Leola." Michael's voice behind me sent a shock wave down my spine, and I gasped in startled awareness that he had entered the room without our knowledge. I spun around to face him, feeling my mouth drop open.

"I couldn't stay away, Leola. Ten minutes after Graf left the city, I got in my car and followed him. I had to see you again and tell you these things myself." He moved across the room toward us. "I just hope I'm not making a fool of myself by doing so."

I shook my head and heard Graf clear his throat.

"So, you really did mean it, man," he said gruffly.

Michael nodded. "I really did." He turned to me. "I'm sorry about how it all went down. I hope we can all start over again..."

Graf still looked confused, but I heard him sigh.

"Look, could we maybe just forget about it for now and try to have a nice Christmas?" He seemed to be grasping at making the best of an awkward situation.

I nodded. I didn't know what else to say. The situation suddenly seemed surreal, but in a good way.

"I saw some gifts under the tree with my name on them," Graf said. "And, I brought one for you, too, Mom."

I was desperate to make the best of the situation, too. I glanced at Michael.

"But, I don't have one for you, Honey," I said softly.

Then Graf laughed lightly. "Oh, yes, you do. That black cashmere sweater? That has Michael's name written all over it."

I snapped a glance at my son. "You looked? You unwrapped and rewrapped the gifts?" I swatted him playfully. "How could you?"

He shrugged. "Mom, I look every year before Christmas. You know that, don't you?"

I just shook my head and grinned at him. I had known that he looked every year. But he'd never admitted it before. I guess it was just another sign of his maturity showing through.

Our Christmas was somehow happy and peaceful after that. It became the first of many the three of us have since spent together. We never again spoke about the awkward way that it had started.

As time went on, my new love blossomed. Michael and I decided to get married a year after that first holiday, and by then, we had

12

Graf's full-hearted blessing. Our lives together have blended together in a way that I never could have imagined, especially since Michael is so much younger than I am. But, that has never been an issue or a problem among us. Our family grows stronger every day. And, we have Graf's maturity that first Christmas to thank for it.

THE END

DESPERATE LOVE
Anything For The Teacher

"Don't tell me you're going back to school, Janine," my best friend Brenetta said. "All those tests would kill me."

I grinned back at her. "I'm sick of settling for low pay. I have a plan."

Brenetta rolled her eyes. "A plan," she said. "Listen to you." After she got over laughing at my admission, she turned and looked me in the eye. "What kind of plan?"

I pulled my legs up beneath me and got comfortable as I settled into discussing what I intended to do with my life. I was going to get my college degree, then go to work at a hospital as a physical therapist. Sure, I knew it wouldn't be easy, but I was smart. There was no reason why I shouldn't give it a shot.

"Where you gonna get the money to live?" she asked.

"The lady in human resources told me I could work the night shift."

"Work all night, go to school all day? When you gonna sleep?"

"I know it won't be easy, but I'm determined. I'm still young enough to make it work."

Brenetta laughed a little more, but I could tell she was beginning to soften a little to my idea. She asked a few questions once she got over the surprise of learning I had plans to better myself.

The very next day I found myself at registration at the local college where I'd applied. It's a small school that specializes in the medical field. They work directly with the hospital.

"Hi, there," a male voice said behind me.

I whipped around and found myself face-to-face with the best looking specimen of a man I'd ever laid eyes on. My heart did a double-time beat, while I stammered to find words that made sense.

He had a short haircut, a pencil-thin mustache, broad shoulders, and the warmest smile I ever saw. And he towered over me.

"Uh, hi," I finally managed to say.

The man continued smiling back at me as he asked me if I needed assistance. I managed to tell him what I was there for, and he nodded.

"I'll probably have you in one of my classes," he said. "I teach freshman English."

My throat had a lump in it. With this man standing at the front of the class, I had no doubt my mind would be somewhere other than where it should be.

14

"My name is Dr. Henderson. Edward Henderson."

I extended my shaky hand. "I'm Janine Sanders," I told him. "I'm looking forward to English."

What a stupid thing to say, I thought as he said a few more nice things then walked away. If I acted this way when I first met the guy, he was bound to expect the worst from me.

"Just think," Brenetta said when I told her how registration went, complete with a play-by-play description of my meeting Dr. Edward Henderson. "With low expectations, he'll be pleasantly surprised at how smart you really are."

"But you don't understand," I cried. "English is my worst subject."

"Then you'll just have to study a little harder for that class. Ask him if he tutors." The sly look on her face let me know she had other things in mind. I laughed.

That night, as I lay in bed thinking about asking Dr. Edward Henderson about tutoring me, I imagined what the session would be like. He'd be sitting across the table from me, books between us, him all serious and me with the hots for him. No way would I be able to concentrate.

If he even so much as touched my hand, I'd probably do something I'd later regret. And don't even think about the two of us being alone in a room together. I couldn't be held accountable for my actions.

All my life I'd been very physical in my relationships. Men either turned me on, or they didn't. If I liked what I saw when I first met them, then I knew something could happen between the man and me. If I didn't like the way they looked, there wasn't a chance.

I definitely liked the way Dr. Henderson looked. And it appeared, based on how he'd looked at me with his eyelids at half-mast, he liked what he saw, too. And if I wasn't imagining things, he'd been flirting with me-just a little.

As I continued thinking about Dr. Henderson, I imagined running my hands down his chest. Although I hadn't seen what he looked like without his clothes on, I still knew he'd be wonderful. Guys like Dr. Edward Henderson had smooth, shiny chests, with possibly only a smattering of hair. It would be rock hard.

My insides sizzled as my imagination continued running away with me. I closed my eyes and allowed the sensation of my thoughts to go crazy. It was wild.

His long, strong fingers would touch me all over, and I'd melt as he entered my body. His smooth motions would drive me absolutely wild with passion, and I'd lift my hips to meet his.

There wouldn't be an inch of space between us as we made love for hours on end. I'd please him, then he'd please me. We'd take turns

15

and gather our strength when we were on the receiving end.

"Oh, Dr. Henderson," I said in a sigh. Then my eyes popped open. I couldn't call him that in the throes of passion. A smile settled on my face as I closed my eyes and said, "Edward." There. That was more like it. Edward in bed; Dr. Henderson in the classroom. No one would ever know.

My imagination was vivid. I was able to feel the pleasure as I thought of showering with Dr. Edward Henderson, both of us covered in lather, sliding our hands all over, enjoying the slipperiness of the soap.

Every time I met a man who turned me on, I found myself doing this. Only this was the first time I'd thought about making it with a teacher—probably because they used to seem so old. But now that I was a mature adult, I was in their league.

I'd just imagined climaxing with Dr. Henderson when I closed my eyes again and fell asleep. My dreams were nothing compared to what I'd thought when awake. This was normal for me.

The days after that seemed to drag. I could hardly wait to start back to school. My first day of classes was less than a week away, and I was a nervous wreck.

There were times when I felt a little self-doubt, but once I pictured Dr. Henderson in my mind, I knew that wild horses couldn't keep me away from that school. I hoped and prayed to have him for English.

And I did. On the first day of school, he was standing at the front of the class, waiting for everyone to be seated. I smiled and said hi to him. He smiled back and said he was glad I was in his class.

I knew he meant it, too. Just the way he looked at me told me he felt something and that it wasn't just my imagination. Of course, it didn't hurt that I'd worn my sexiest red skirt and white knit shirt that dipped low in front and showed cleavage. I saw his eyes as they darted to my chest and then back to my eyes. What I saw on his face was pure, unadulterated appreciation.

"Hi, my name's Dr. Henderson," he informed us once the class was all seated. "I hope to teach you the classics this semester. If there's anything you don't understand, please let me know, and I'll do my best to help you. Since this is a small class, I can give you some one-on-one attention."

I felt my heart pounding as he said that. Was he looking directly at me, or was that my imagination running wild again?

As I took notes during class, I had to focus on what I was writing rather than looking at him like I really wanted to do. He was wearing a polo shirt and dark khaki slacks that gave him a country club golfer look. And it suited him just fine. In fact, I had a feeling that Dr. Edward Henderson would look good in anything he wore.

He kept us in the class for the entire period. Afterwards, I got up, slowly picked up my books and purse, and made it a point to be the last student to leave.

"Hi, Ms. Sanders," he said as I brushed past him.

I turned around and acted like I hadn't noticed him standing there. "Hi, Dr. Henderson."

I tried to think of something else to say, but nothing would come out of my mouth. We were standing so close, I could feel that familiar energy as it sizzled through my body.

His smile was still warm, but it was more familiar now. And those eyes of his melted me from the inside out.

"Don't hesitate to ask for help if you need it," he told me.

I looked at him coyly as I tilted my head to one side. "Are you sure you don't mind?"

He chuckled, a low, husky sound that nearly turned me inside out. "Of course I don't mind. I wouldn't have offered if I did mind."

That sounded like a come-on to me. I smiled back at him and lifted my shoulders. "Well, I better run on to my next class so I'm not late. See you later, Dr. Henderson."

He nodded, smiled again, and watched as I left. I wondered what was on his mind. Could he possibly be thinking the same thing I was?

I sat through a history class and then college algebra. With the exception of freshman English, I hated the fact that I had to take all these core classes just to get my degree in physical therapy.

Once I was finished for the day, I rushed home, took a quick nap, got up, showered, and ate some leftovers. I had to be at work soon, and I wouldn't be back home until the wee hours of the morning when I'd have to grab another nap. This schedule would be grueling, but at least it wasn't forever. And I'd wind up with a much better life because of it.

My classes only met three days a week, which gave me the chance to do my schoolwork to prepare for the next day. It took me several weeks to get used to the routine, but eventually, I was able to feel human once I got into the swing of things. My naps were valuable to me, and I didn't allow myself to miss one because I knew if I did, I wouldn't be worth two cents.

Dr. Henderson had jumped right into the material, and it took everything I had to keep up with him. He rattled off the subject matter so fast, I almost couldn't keep up. Some of the students had resorted to using tape recorders.

One of the things I enjoyed doing when he took a break between lectures was watching his face light up over what he was teaching. I could tell he thoroughly enjoyed what he did for a living, something that made him even sexier. But now, I was just too tired and too busy to do anything about it.

17

We were almost three weeks into the semester when I finally realized I'd missed a whole chunk of material in English. Dr. Henderson had said something important while I was racing to keep up with his notes.

Since he'd made the offer to help me if I needed it, I felt like now was a good time to take him up on it. I still thought he was sexy, but my role as student and his as instructor had become more defined, and I wasn't quite as comfortable as I thought I'd be.

"Uh, Dr. Henderson," I said as I walked up to him after class, "I have a question."

"Yes, Ms. Sanders," he said as he put his pencil down on the desk and turned to me. "What can I help you with?"

He folded his arms over his chest, which made his biceps more defined. I had to swallow the lump in my throat before I could speak.

"I hate to admit this, but I missed a whole five minutes of your lecture," I told him.

Dr. Henderson laughed. "Am I that boring?"

"No," I gasped. "Not at all."

"I understand you're burning the candle at both ends. Maybe you should slow down just a little."

Suddenly, I felt defensive. "It's not that. I just can't write as fast as you can talk."

He slowly nodded his understanding. "Why don't you stop by my office around three o'clock this afternoon? You don't have a class then, do you?"

"No," I said. But I did need to get some sleep, and that was the time I generally did it. "I'll be there."

He gave me instructions on how to find him, then I left. Hopefully, I'd be able to get my notes and leave. My attraction to him was still there, but I was mature enough to know better than to do something stupid.

At least I thought I was.

Once I got to the door of Dr. Henderson's office, I felt my knees go weak at the sight of him. He was sitting at a desk, his head bent down over some papers, his forehead crinkled in concentration, and a pencil in his right hand, poised as if he might use it at any moment. I could tell he was a brilliant and studious man, which I found very sexy.

I slowly lifted my hand and knocked on the open door. He quickly glanced up. Once he spotted me, a slow smile spread over his lips, which made me feel special. That look was just for me.

"Hi, Ms. Sanders." He stood up. "Come on in and close the door behind you."

My heart kept hammering harder and harder in my chest as I did

18

as I was told. When I turned around, though, Dr. Henderson was still sitting at his desk.

"What can I help you with?" he asked as he leaned back and rubbed his chin with his thumb and index finger.

"I, uh, I didn't get the whole lecture this morning. I was wondering if you could give me your notes."

I watched as he pulled his bottom lip between his teeth. He seemed to be thinking about more than just giving me notes.

"Yes," he finally said, "that can be arranged. Would you like them now, or would you like to have them over dinner?"

"Dinner?" I said.

He smiled as he leaned over his desk, coming close enough for me to see his pupils dilate. "Yes, I was thinking it would be nice to have dinner together some evening soon."

"Is that okay?" I asked, wishing I'd just gone along with him and accepted.

He shrugged. "I guess it might be misconstrued if anyone from the department or any of the other students knew about it." With a brief pause, he added, "But if we're discreet I don't see the problem."

I nodded. "I can be discreet. I won't say a word to anyone."

It was impossible to keep the excitement from my voice. Here was the man of my dreams asking me out to dinner. So what if he was my teacher. I could separate the two.

"Good. How's tomorrow?"

"Perfect," I said.

I gave him directions to my place, and he told me when he'd pick me up. "Wear something nice," he told me. "I'd like to take you to a very special place."

This was turning out even better than I thought. My teacher was not only giving me the class notes, he was taking me out to dinner, and he said it was a special place. That had to mean something.

The next day dragged by. I studied all the notes I had, and I made a spot in my notebook for the ones I planned to get from Dr. Henderson.

Then it dawned on me. What should I call him?

If we were seeing each other, should I continue to call him Dr. Henderson? Or should I call him Edward? Maybe he went by Ed.

My nicest dress was one with blue sequins on the bodice and a silky skirt. It enhanced the bronze coloring of my skin and showed off all my attributes, especially my cleavage. The skirt skimmed my thighs and made me feel really pretty.

Apparently, Dr. Henderson thought so, too. He grinned at me and nodded, his eyebrows raised.

"You look absolutely breathtaking," he said. This was the first time any man had ever put it that way. It was like in the movies.

We were on our way to the restaurant when he turned to me and said, "Please stop the Dr. Henderson business. Most of my friends just call me Eddie."

"Eddie?" I said. "Are you sure?"

"Honey, you can call me whatever you want, but people will think it's strange when I hold you and you're calling me Dr. Henderson."

I let out an audible sigh. He laughed.

Reaching out to take my hand, he said, "And if you don't mind, I'd like to call you Janine."

"Oh, yeah, that's fine." I gulped. "Eddie."

The restaurant where he took me was a very quiet little Italian place on the other side of town. It was dimly lit, but everyone there seemed to recognize him.

"Eddie," the host said as we walked into the dining room, "where ya been?"

"Working hard, Mario," Eddie said.

The host looked at me, smiled from beneath his wide mustache, and nodded. "Yes, I see that. Where would you and the lady like to sit?"

I felt so important being with Dr. Edward Henderson. He was obviously well known and respected. The service was impeccable, leading me to believe he was a regular at the place.

"How's the meal?" he asked.

"I love it. How did you ever find this place?" I asked.

Eddie chuckled. "I'm part owner."

I nearly choked on my food. "You own this place?"

With a nod, Eddie replied, "Yeah, my dad and Mario were old friends. I grew up thinking he was an uncle or something. Mario has worked here since he was a kid. Anyway, when this place came up for sale, he tried to talk my dad into going into business with him, but my dad turned him down."

"How did you get involved?" I asked.

With a shrug, Eddie said, "I always appreciated good food, and I loved Mario like an uncle. So I figured it was time to diversify and set up something on the side for retirement."

"Do you work here, too?" I asked.

"No. In fact, they refuse to let me in the kitchen. I'm like a bull in a china cabinet."

I laughed. "So you're a silent partner."

"Yeah, the money guy."

Mario was at our table by now, asking what we'd like for dessert. He turned to me. "We have the best tiramasu, if I say so myself."

Eddie nodded. "It's the best."

Tiramisu sounded wonderful, but I was stuffed. I held my waist as I shook my head. "Maybe next time I won't eat so much. I'm too full now."

Mario grinned from ear to ear, making his mustache look like a caterpillar crawling across his face. "Next time, huh?" He looked at Eddie. "You better bring this girl back. She's pretty."

"Don't worry, Mario," Eddie said, "I will."

Once Mario had left the table, Eddie reached out and took my hand. I grinned back at him and enjoyed the feeling I had. It was a combination of contentment and sexual excitement, since we still had the rest of the evening to enjoy. I didn't have to go in to work tonight, so I could stay out as late as I wanted.

"Do you need to go home now?" he asked.

"No," I replied.

Eddie licked his lips as he stood and pulled me to my feet. We walked arm in arm out the door with Mario standing staring after us. I knew we looked good together, and it felt great.

"Wanna go to my place?" he asked.

"Sure."

"Or better yet, why don't we go to the East Park?"

The East Park was a large, heavily treed and shrubbed place on one side of the biggest lake in town. There were picnic tables and benches all over the place, and it had the reputation for being a perfect makeout spot for lovers.

"I'd love to."

Eddie drove to East Park with me sitting by his side. I felt like I had the world by the tail when I was with this man.

Once we got there and parked, he led me to a bench hidden between two trees. We had a lovely view of the lake, but no one else could see us unless they were standing less than five feet from us. It was very private.

My breath caught in my throat as Eddie gently placed his arm around my shoulders. I leaned into him and felt my body tingle as his rock hard chest came into contact with my side.

"Janine," he whispered.

I turned to him in time for his lips to meet mine. With tender pecks, he planted tiny kisses on my lips, across my cheeks, over my nose, my eyelids, and down my throat. A low moan escaped my throat.

"I want to make you feel good, Janine," he whispered.

"Oh, Eddie, I feel so good."

Eddie reached out and tugged at the spaghetti straps of my dress, pulling them down my shoulders and arms, baring my breasts. "You're beautiful, Janine."

"Oh, Eddie," I moaned.

"I want to feel you close to me."

I reached out and began to undo his buttons, one by one, until he was bare-chested, too. Then he pulled me into his arms and began to stroke my back.

"What if someone sees us?" I asked when we were both totally naked from the waist up.

"No one will see us. This is a very private spot. Besides, it's night time, and this place is deserted."

I turned my face up to his for more kisses. As he sucked on my bottom lip, he undid the zipper at the back of my dress. It slid to the ground.

"Stand up, Janine," he begged. "I want to see all of you."

All I wore now were my four-inch spike heels. I felt self-conscious, but I did as he asked. The only light we had was the moon.

"You're wonderful, Janine." He nipped at my lip and pulled back again. "And delicious."

As he held me close again, I could feel his erection. That let me know he was experiencing the same sensations I was. And it turned me on even more.

He pulled back for a moment and looked at me. His eyes were narrowed, and his jaw was tight. I could tell he was holding back.

"Don't stop," I begged.

"Are you sure?" he asked. "I don't want to take advantage of you, Janine."

"Positive," I said. "Don't make me hurt you."

"Hurt me?"

I yanked him closer as I unzipped his pants, springing him from the constraints that had kept us apart for more minutes than I could comfortably bear. To my surprise and delight, he wasn't wearing any underwear. I was even more stimulated than before, if that was possible.

"I want you," I stated firmly.

He laughed as he slid my skirt up to pull my thighs apart and thrust himself inside me. "I certainly don't want to make you beg, Janine. Here I am."

My legs went weak as we moved together, thrusting and pulling, tugging and pushing. If anyone had been watching, I didn't care. All I cared about was how Eddie made me feel. I wanted more. I couldn't get enough.

Finally, when he was spent, I held him close. "Are you satisfied?" he asked.

"For now."

With a grin, he helped me get my clothes back like they were before he dressed himself. Always the gentleman.

"I hope you don't have any regrets later," he told me.

I shrugged. "Why should I?"

"Well, for one thing," he said slowly, "I'm the teacher, and you're my student."

I began to laugh. "Exactly what is it you're teaching?"

Eddie smiled. "Whatever you want to learn, m'dear."

We bantered all the way back to his car and then he drove me home. As we sat in the parking lot below my apartment, he turned me to face him.

"You do realize we either have to stop seeing each other, or you have to be transferred to another English class, right?"

"Why?"

Eddie hung his head. He couldn't seem to look at me as he spoke.

"Because I live by a very strict code of ethics. If there's any chance of anything being unethical, I don't want any part of it."

My heart twisted. "Is there another English class?"

"There's one," he replied, "but it meets at a different time."

"What would you like for me to do?" I asked.

He shrugged. "I'd like to see you again, but I can't make your decision for you."

"Let me think about it," I told him. "In the meantime, I'd like to get those notes I first came to you about."

Eddie snapped his fingers. "Oh, yeah, that's right. I almost forgot."

As he reached over to get the papers from the back seat, I studied his physique. This was one hot man, but even I knew that wasn't enough. I wanted to be independent, even if I did wind up falling in love and settling down eventually. My first goal had to be my education.

My heart ached as I thought about the timing of getting involved with Eddie. I wanted him more than almost anything. Anything, that is, but my education that would pull me out of the low-paying jobs I'd had to work since high school. Surely, he'd understand. Afterwards, there would be time. Yes, I knew there was the risk of Eddie finding someone else and losing my own chance with him, but that risk was one I needed to take. I'd seen too many people put everything on one man, only to be left later with nothing but memories. I wanted more from life.

He walked me to my door, then I went to the window and watched him drive away. There went the most magnificent man I'd ever made love with. I wanted more nights like this with the man who was able to drive me straight to ecstasy with one look. But I still wasn't sure about an ongoing relationship with him.

From what I'd heard, he was one of the best instructors at the school. In fact, I didn't even know about another professor of English, since everyone was always talking about Dr. Henderson's class. And

I didn't want to risk my education simply for passion that could fade at any minute.

As much as I wanted to continue to see him for my physical needs, I knew exactly what I had to do. The question was, should I back off without saying anything, or should I have a talk with him?

If I didn't say anything, he would probably wonder what was wrong. I wasn't mad or anything. He might get the wrong idea.

However, if I made it a point to talk to him, he might try to encourage me to stick around and see what happens in our relationship. That would have been fine if I hadn't made a promise to myself.

I agonized over my decision until it was time to go to class again. And I knew what I had to do.

After class was over, I lingered in the room until the last of the students had left. When it was just Eddie and me, I looked at him and nodded. He motioned for me to follow him.

We went straight to his office where he closed the door behind me. I turned around to find myself in his arms. He was about to kiss me.

Man, I wanted that kiss more than anything I could imagine. But I pulled away. He frowned down at me.

"Janine, are you mad at me?" he asked.

"No, Eddie," I said slowly, "but we do need to talk. Please sit down. This won't be easy."

With a deep frown on his face, Eddie went around behind his desk and sat down. I sat across from him. We stared at each other for a few seconds before I began.

"I can't remember ever feeling so alive as I felt when we made love a few nights ago," I told him. "And I'd be lying if I said I didn't want to do it again."

He held both hands up and shook his head. "Then what's the problem? You can get switched out of my class, and we can go on seeing each other."

"No, that's the problem, Eddie. I don't want to get switched out of your class. You're the best English teacher in the school, and I want a good education."

Eddie started to smile, but then what I said sank in. He made a grumbling sound.

I continued telling him how everyone wanted to be in his class and that I'd never learned so much or been so excited about great literature. When I finally stood to leave, he thanked me.

"I never thought I'd regret being a good teacher," he said, "but I guess that's better than the alternative."

"You're the best," I said. "Don't ever regret it."

He let out a deep sigh. "Okay, Janine, we can hold off until the end of the semester, but will you at least think about giving us another shot once there's no chance I'll ever teach one of your classes?"

With a wide grin on my face, I nodded. My heart sang. Maybe there was hope.

"Absolutely," I replied with a smile.

Eddie came around from behind the desk, opened his arms wide, and motioned with his head for me to come to him. I reluctantly did it, knowing what a magnetic pull his body had for mine. But we just hugged. Nothing else.

After I left Eddie's office, I had to hurry to get to my next class. I sat there in a daze, wondering if I'd done the right thing. But deep in my heart I knew I had.

If what Eddie and I felt for each other was real, we could resume the relationship later. The feelings would still be there. And we'd both be free to pursue whatever happened naturally because I'd never have to depend on him for anything other than the romance.

THE END

FATAL LOVE
If I Couldn't Have Him, No One Could!

Turning to look at Nassir, I found him looking at me. For just a second my heart stopped beating. With his lightly crooked smile there was something dangerously primitive about this man. Regardless, when I felt Nassir's hand on my shoulder, I did not pull away. Slowly, I turned to face him.

Unable to draw away even as any initial fright receded, the strength of his body was critical. I relaxed against him. Stealing precious moments of support as I might a forbidden elegance.

Nassir flinched, as though something inside him had snapped. "Shhh!" He brought a hand to my mouth. Nassir cupped my face with his hands.

I gave myself up to his kiss because he touched something raw within me, something that all the protest in the world couldn't deny. Nassir's lips opened agonizingly over mine, touching me, draining me until the thirst was mutual and demanding. His tongue thrust deeply, singeing mine, matching its length, then drawing it into his own mouth. When his arms left my back to frame my face, I planted my feet firmly on the ground. Only then did Nassir lips release mine, leaving my mouth burning with fire.

I gasped when he took advantage of my ridged state. Sliding his hand to encircle my breast, he moaned softly. "Oh God, Abena. You're so firm, so full."

His hand gently fondled me, his thumb finding then teasing the tip of my nipple. I sighed a deeper breath and closed my eyes, arching my back. My legs were beginning to tremble but I could no more have removed myself from him than I could have denied, at that second the very obvious proof of my arousal. Nassir picked me up into his arms.

"Come here," he said, hauling me higher until his lips touched the fullness of my breast. Through the fabric of my shirt he nibbled at my flesh. His tongue dampened the silk blouse, sending a fiery heat through my skin toward my most feminine core. I nodded, dumbly aware that my finger remained on his chest until he grabbed my hand and pressed it to his heart, inching it downward and around the muscled swell of his erection. His chest was firm beneath my palm, his heartbeat much more steady than my own. When my fingertip grazed his tight nipple my gaze shot to his.

Lost in a world of exquisite pleasure, I sighed his name, "Nassir." I lowered my head and buried my face in his hair, breathing deeply of his clean male scent. Through vague remnants of lucidity, I wondered how anyone could smell so clean after working for the better part of the day.

Then I realized that what struck my senses was the sheer maleness of Nassir. Chemistry wise, he could do no wrong. Intention wise, not so. Suddenly, he was whirling action, fighting with the darkness for something I could fathom. His hands tugged my shirt up high enough to allow his hand to caress my breast. I never dreamed his hands would feel so warm, so gentle.

"What are you doing?" I gasped, twisting his hands and anchored them to my chest. "No" I cried then lowered my voice to a husky whisper. "No, It's wrong."

He was breathing heavily. I had felt the rapid rise and fall of his chest. I had felt what he did.

"Abena, I'm not taking 'no' for an answer until you've given me a fair change to get a 'yes'. You love me and I know it. Conrad is gone. You need to put the past behind us."

I went on breathlessly holding his hands all the more tightly, fearful of what might happen should he touch me again. For seconds I stayed in his embrace, registering the strong beat of his heart, and the faint scent of his aftershave.

Nassir stood abruptly, leaning over, pulling me gently to him. "This isn't the place or time," he said burying his face in my hair as he groaned. "I'm going to touch you again, Abena. Not now. But later." His husky whisper held a shadow of desperation. "I'm going to touch you, kiss you and do everything I've only been able to lie awake at night imagining. I'll make you want me so badly that you'll never remember there was another man in the world. Then I'm going to make love to you, over and over again in ways you never dreamed."

Scrupulously, I straightened my vest, putting it down toward my waist, over my silk shirt.

Suddenly the silence was interrupted by a loud sound from the other side of the house. It was followed by a yell loud enough to assure me, that we were as yet undiscovered.

"You-hoo" a voice proclaimed from beyond. "You-hoo is anybody home?" I said a silent prayer for the voice. Aunt Myrna coming home was a godsend. Nassir's direct words had a disturbing effect on me.

I walked away from him that afternoon. My mind and body were finally moving together.

"Oh, you're here Nassir," Aunt Myrna said. "Will you be staying for dinner?"

"I'm sorry Aunt Myrna," I replied. "Nassir has plans for tonight." My voice was absolutely emotionless and it chilled me. It didn't help that Nassir was not six feet from me. Nor did it help that each time I dared a glance at him he met my gaze.

Aunt Myrna looked at Nassir without saying a word. The conversation seemed to have come to an awkward end and I wished Nassir would leave. Nassir echoed, "I must be going."

"Isn't Nassir a wonderful man," Aunt Myrna said.

That was all I needed. I was in no mood to talk about Nassir or any man. I felt a churning in my stomach.

"Aunt Myrna, I'm going to lay down for a minute," I said. I went into the bedroom.

I wasn't entitled to find love. I once knew all the contentment and satisfaction most girls dream of. Nassir had no right to think he could take Conrad's place.

I was Conrad's widow. Everyone was saying "Abena is so brave." Inside me, I was slowly dying for the sound of Conrad's voice.

I will always wonder if Conrad had a premonition. Did he know that our time together would be so short? And yet what could have warned him? We had seven wonderful years together and a future looked bright.

As I put my story down on paper, even after three years, it is like tearing my heart out with each word. But I want to tell my story for other women like me, too numb with grief to think straight, too broken and crushed by the loss of their loved ones to face the future alone.

The two people that made my world were wiped out like the bat of an eye. One day we were all together, our lives closely interwoven in a pattern of love and companionship. Then abruptly I was alone. All alone. Conrad was dead and my little daughter, Katha, with him.

Conrad and I grew up together in New Albany, a small town located about thirty miles from Louisville with a population about 5,000. His mother had died when he was eleven and he lived across the street from me with his Aunt Myrna who had brought him up.

We shared practically every day of our lives, except for the time Conrad went away to the Gulf War. Then I knew what it was to live in fear and apprehension. I had my first step of loneliness.

That feeling was for me to face alone, seven years later. That's how long Conrad and I had to be together, but mercifully we didn't know. We believed, like any other couple who love each other, that we had all eternity.

"You'll make such a cute mother," Conrad used to say before we even had little Katha. Then I'd kiss his lips, and there would be nothing but compassion. It was enough. We never needed anything else, or asked for more.

Conrad brought back something from the war other than

28

photographs and souvenirs. He brought Nassir Lucas, his buddy. I'd heard about Nassir in all of Conrad's letters—about his homeliness, his heart of gold, his lack of any family, his humor and kindness. When I met him, I found that Conrad hadn't exaggerated.

"I love you today, Abena," he whispered, and I nuzzled my cheek against his warm brown neck a moment.

"I love you too, Conrad," I answered.

The day went along as usual. The hours not long enough for all I wanted to do. By 5:30 our back yard was full of the crowd who had come for our last cookout of the season. It was like dozens of others we'd had in the past, around the little outdoor fireplace Conrad had built.

There were half a dozen young couples, most of whom Conrad and I had gone to school with. Conrad put his arm around me. For a moment we danced in silence, moving like one to the slow rhythm. Then Conrad said the strangest thing, the thing that haunts me to this day.

"You know, Abena, if anything ever happened to me, I wouldn't want you to be alone. Some people could take it, but you shouldn't. It would hurt to think of someone else holding you but it's the way I'd want it to be if I couldn't be with you-"

He stopped suddenly, pulled me close to him and whispered "Honey, I've made you cry. I'm sorry. I only said what popped in my head. Forget it, darling-"

I did forget it, until less than twenty-four hours later. Just before we left the club, Nassir told Conrad, "I'll pick you and Katha up at nine tomorrow. That's not too early, is it?"

"It's fine," Conrad said. "We'll take the outboard motor along, so we won't lose time getting down to the south end of the lake. If we make a haul, you can bring both of your girl friends over for a fish fry in the back yard tomorrow night."

"Melody doesn't like fish," Nassir chuckled. "I'll bring Wilma."

Later that night, after Conrad had taken Aunt Myrna home, we stood together in Katha's room, looking at her. She lay sprawled and relaxed in the wide bed.

"She looks like an angel asleep," I whispered, a lump in my throat. "Oh, Conrad, I hope she has a good life. I hope she does something useful and worthwhile in the world."

He took my hand and we went into our bedroom. One corner of his mouth was turned up in amusement as his eyes met mine. Then his gaze traveled lazily back over my body, taking in the soft swell of my breasts beneath the high cut teddy. His hand moved down touching one silken length of my legs. Conrad's eyes lingered on my breasts, then rose to meet my wide-eyed gaze.

I felt my insides turn to the consistency of maple syrup when he reached out and touched my face. His nearness and the wonderful very muscular smell of his cologne made me dizzy with desire. When he ran his fingers through my hair and pulled me into his embrace. My knees threatened to collapse like a folding chair.

In my excitement, I moved against him before guiding him inside me. My legs clamped firmly against his. I moved slowly up and down until I could no longer hear the glorious heat of desire. My movements became faster and faster until both our passions were spent. My head fell against his neck as a sob of ecstasy escaped my lips.

And then with a gentle push he was inside me once more. A moan burst from my lips as the tempo of his thrusts became faster. I surrendered to a thrilling climax that left me limp. I slept in his arms that last night, as I had slept all the other nights we had together. The room was bright with daylight when I half awoke. Conrad and Katha were trying to kiss me good-by quietly. I remember the feel of Katha's warm round arms, the soft pressure of her little lips on mine.

"Good by mommy. We'll being you lots and lots of fish.

"Let's go," Conrad said. "Uncle Nassir is out front waiting."

I lifted my lips drowsily for Conrad's kiss.

"Go back to sleep, pumpkin," he said, pulling the sheet up under my chin. "Dream about me while I'm gone."

I was asleep again before the sound of the car died away in the distance. It was ten o'clock when I sat straight up in bed, curiously wide-awake. I thought I'd heard Katha calling urgently, "Mommy! Mommy!" and Troubles barking excitedly. But when I ran to the window to look out into the morning, no car was in front of the house. I lifted my arms above my head, breathed in the fresh air and stretched from sheer exuberance. It was such a wonderful morning.

I hurried dressing. My husband and child would be back before too long. Yet, I had time to start the roast. They still hadn't come and I felt apprehension.

Mid-afternoon I walked to the mailbox. When I started back to the house I saw Nassir coming down the street. But he was alone. When Nassir got out of the car his face looked gray and he moved like an old man.

"Abena, let's go in the house," his lips said but I heard no sound. I walked after him, and now I walked strangely, too like a person asleep. Because suddenly I knew that something had happened. I knew it was something terrible and that in a few moments I was going to know what it was.

Nassir's face was blurred and wavered before me. His voice was like no voice I had ever heard before hoarse, and stumbling with horror.

30

"I wanted to tell you myself," he said. "I didn't want anyone else to do it. Conrad and Katha—there's been an accident, Abena. They're-"

I think he knew that if anyone else told me, I wouldn't have believed it.

"The outboard motor went haywire, and the boat went crazy and capsized-"

Nassir's eyes were blank with shock. "They drowned," I said slowly and distinctly, reasoning it out, word by word. "They're dead. Conrad and Katha are dead."

"Yes, Abena-"

"I'm all right. I'm not going to faint. I'll be all right." I turned my back and walked to the kitchen.

That was the last thing I remembered clearly for close to a week. Yet I moved through those days calmly, made the decisions I had to, answered the shocked, pitying words of neighbors and friends. I didn't break. I didn't sleep. Because if I slept, I would have to awaken and realize all over again that the only two people in my world were dead. I stayed with Aunt Myrna. They wouldn't let me go home. I asked Nassir to attend to everything. Nassir had seen Conrad and Katha drown before his eyes, while he frantically tried to save them. It had been hardest for Nassir, but I didn't realize that then.

Now I remember that his eyes were tear-filled the day of the funeral, but I was too sunken in my own grief to notice then. Now I remember, too, that as I knelt by the gravestone that marked the resting-place of my loved ones he said, "I wish it had been me, instead."

I didn't answer him. Why hadn't it been Nassir instead of Katha or Conrad? Selfishly, ruthlessly I agreed with him. I hated him for being alive. But I must be very careful what I thought. The only thing to do was to hold my thoughts as still as possible until after the funeral, until everything required of me had been done.

The only way to hold your thoughts still is to put them on the people around you. I watched the people who came and went, offering their sympathy, their services.

"If anything ever happened to me-" Conrad's voice was as clear in my ears as if he had spoken. In my thoughts we were together again, moving like one across the dance floor.

At the funeral, I sat between Aunt Myrna, broken and weeping, and Nassir, still as a church mouse. There were two gray caskets in the church heaped with flowers. Someone was playing a hymn on the organ, but I didn't recognize it.

Reverend Williams face was blurred, just as Nassir's had been that fatal day. He spoke gibberish. I heard someone sob. I looked blankly toward the altar. None of the beauty around me meant anything. If

I didn't leave, I would stand up and tell Reverend Williams before everybody how God had laughed at me. But if I left people would be shocked. They'd say I wasn't showing respect for Conrad and Katha. I put my hand on Nassir's arm.

"I must leave," I said quietly. "Right now, Nassir." Outside it was still August but bleak and windy like winter.

I shivered and pulled my coat closer about me. "Let's walk to the cemetery," I said.

As we walked along, I kept talking almost as if to myself. "I want to see them covered. Maybe then I will understand that it's over. That will be all. There won't be anything after that." Nassir didn't say a word.

After a while I said, "The numbness is wearing off in places a few minutes at a time, Nassir. What will I do when all the numbness is gone?"

"I'd give my life if I could make this easier for you, Abena," Nassir answered. "But I don't know what to tell you that would help."

"Poor thing, if you could cry!" Nancy Anderson said beside me. "Abena come over to the house later if you feel the need to be with some one."

"Thank you," I said politely. I was only half listening. That night I told Aunt Myrna and Nassir my plans to leave town.

"I'm going home in the morning and start doing the things that have to be done," I finished. "I don't want anyone to help me."

I went home very early the next morning. It was another gray, cloudy day and not many people were stirring so early. "Why?" I cried out. "Why has God chosen to hurt me so?" What Conrad and I had had, we had fashioned ourselves, from our love. Now the pattern was gone, the love broken and destroyed and nothing was left but a horrible vacuum in which I must struggle for sanity.

I unlocked the door and walked straight back into the memories. Katha's baseball bat stood beside Conrad's golf clubs. I stood listening. Any minute the two of them might burst in the door, back from their fishing trip.

The agony of emotions is worse than any physical torture. I stumbled to my knees and laid my head on Conrad's recliner. At this moment my heart and my whole being at last realized the complete finality of death.

Conrad and Katha were not anywhere. They were not in this house that had been so alive with laughter and love four days ago. Out of the darkness, I heard a sound, steps on the porch, and then Nassir's quiet voice.

"Abena, please—I have to talk to you."

I got slowly to my feet. I saw Nassir very clearly.

"Yes, Nassir. What is it?" I asked.

He didn't sit in Conrad's chair. If he had, I would have screamed at him. He sat in another chair, and I sat down, too, and folded my hands in my lap and waited.

"I want you to know," Nassir said, "that half of the newspaper assets are rightfully yours. You won't have to worry about-"

"No," I cut in. "That newspaper was Conrad's hard work and faith. Nothing is mine." There was enough insurance to take care of funeral expenses. "I'll work things out for myself. I want nothing!"

"I guess I'm the last one to help you," he said miserably. "Maybe later I can do something. When time has-"

"Don't tell me time will heal!" I cried furiously. "Five, ten years form now my grief will be as sharp as it is now. I don't want to hear clichés 'Time will heal all wounds. Now please go, Nassir. You were Conrad's friend. I'm trying not to hurt you."

I didn't look at him again. By the time he reached the door, I had forgotten him. I couldn't bear to go on staying in this town.

"If I stay in New Albany, I'll lose my mind!" I told Aunt Myrna.

Finally she confessed, "I'm not well, Abena. I need you." I looked Aunt Myrna straight in the eyes.

"I'm not staying in this town one day longer than I have to." After that she said no more. I went to Louisville. In a city you can be anonymous.

In a city there are only strange faces, none of them with pity. I wasn't seeking beauty, only oblivion. I didn't care that the studio apartment I found was shabby and ugly. I sat in it for days, trying to look at the fact of my own existence.

But the thought stayed. Conrad would want me to find someone else. Something he had said the last night. "Abena, if anything ever happened to me, I wouldn't want you to be alone." When he had said that, he hadn't realized how utterly impossible it would be for me ever to find someone to take his place, to even partly fill the hole he had left in my heart.

I thought of Aunt Myrna and sent her a card. I gave no address where she could write me. I still wanted no contact with any one in New Albany. I found a job at the Project Care-Lake Land College. I answer the telephone and work as a receptionist.

When Keith Humes, a salesman that frequented my office asked me to go on a date with him, I said, "Yes, dinner Wednesday night would be nice."

He came to my apartment that evening carrying a bottle of wine and a bouquet of daisies. I could tell he was pleased with himself. We were soon on our way to dinner. I was aware of his good looks and his strong lean body. I was excited. I had longings I hadn't felt in quite some time. I kept reminding myself that it was a simple dinner invitation.

I yawned, reminding us both of the hour. "I should get you home soon," he said. Approaching my apartment door I said, "Thank you for convincing me to go out tonight. I had a lovely dinner."

Inside my apartment door, I flicked on the light turning to ask if he wanted a cup of coffee. He took an abrupt step toward me.

Keith reached out and pulled me closer. I could feel the hardness of his chest and the beating of his heart. He lowered his head and kissed me firm and hard. My body pressed up against the wall. My back ached because of the awkward position but my body went limp.

"I know you want me," he said. I swallowed hard against the painful lump that raised in my throat. I could tell he meant it as he had never meant anything in his life. I was aware of the fact, aware of the tension in his hands gripping my arm.

"No," I began protesting. Keith stood absolutely still. Then I guess I had said something that really ticked him off because he suddenly grabbed me.

Both of my hands flew up at once toward my face. Before I could react Keith's voice become louder "I'll make you feel good inside," he said.

I wiggled my body around and made a dash for the front door. I ran outside trembling. Keith was not far behind. "Please, leave me alone," I pleaded as we both stood outside my front door. I was ready to scream, awake the neighbors, run down the street if need be. Anything but stay with this man.

My legs were shaky and my body stiffened, but I walked toward my apartment and locked the door behind me. I don't know how long I stood there, staring into space and trembling uncontrollably. Afraid of moving and finding it difficult to breathe. A wave of nausea swept over me just thinking of what had happened.

Doubts and fears drained my body. I was worried and decided to look for other work so I wouldn't have to face Keith Humes at my desk again.

I began to scan the want ads to look for work. That's how I happened to see the small insertion from which my own name leaped out at me. Anyone knowing the whereabouts of Abena Jackson, possibly staying in New Albany, please contact Nassir Lucas . A relative of Mrs. Jackson is seriously ill. I had no relative but Aunt Myrna! Aunt Myrna must be sick—maybe dying. How could I have turned my back of her when she needed me? I owed her so much.

It was the first time I had let the bitterness recede enough to discover what else was left in my empty heart. Immediately I called Nassir at the newspaper office. When I heard the relief in his voice, tears filled my eyes. "Abena, thank heaven you saw that ad! It was a long shot, the only way I could think of to reach you. Can you come? Aunt Myrna needs you."

The tears kept coming, deep sobs and releasing. "I can come, Nassir. What it is?"

"Cancer," he said. "She scared. She refuses to have an operation. She needs you—you're all she has."

"I'll be in New Albany this evening," I whispered in a choked voice. "Tell her I'm coming."

Aunt Myrna needed me. She was the first person who had needed me since my family had gone. A feeling of quiet peace stole over me. I would go to her with sympathy and love in my heart.

As I drove to New Albany I saw the familiar streets and my heart seemed to be opening slowly, letting in old memories with quiet acceptance. They were good memories, gentle memories. Why had I been afraid to face them?

Nassir met me as I got of my car that night and the sight of his familiar figure was oddly comforting. I was glad to see him. I didn't even mind the searching way his gray eyes studied my face.

"You're too thin, Abena," he said gruffly, taking my arm. "What have you been doing to yourself? But the important thing is that you're here. Aunt Myrna has really brightened since I told her you were coming."

I was shocked at how frail Aunt Myrna looked. But her smile was polished as she clung to my hands.

"Abena, child, bless you for coming," she said softly. "I've been so lonely without you, and so frightened. But I won't be afraid now."

"I won't leave you again," I promised.

The thing that hurt inside was that I had left Aunt Myrna alone in the first place. Conrad had been like her own son and she had loved him as much as I had. My child had been like a grandchild to her. Yet I had left her alone with a grief and loss as sharp as mine.

Soon after my arrival in New Albany, Aunt Myrna scheduled her operation. Her chances were slightly less than even, the doctor told us. She went calmly to her operation when the hour came.

While Nassir and I waited at the hospital, he talked of things that had been going on in New Albany since I'd left. I was surprised that it didn't hurt to hear him talk about he past, that I was glad to have news of all our old friends.

Finally they wheeled Aunt Myrna back to her room, an efficient-looking nurse by her side, with her fingers on Aunt Myrna's pulse. I sat still as long as I could, then I paced the corridor with Nassir. Together we walked to the waiting room but I knew I couldn't rest.

I turned suddenly to Nassir, my hand tense on his arm. "She's got to get well, Nassir," I cried. She could show me how to live again, how to be useful and find peace.

Nassir guided me gently to a chair, held one of my hands in his as he sat beside me.

35

"Abena, I've just been getting straightened out on my thinking, too, the past few months. What happened last fall nearly floored me, just as it did you. Because part of my trouble was that I love you, and I felt guilty. I had a mixed-up idea that maybe I was being punished for falling in love with my best friend's wife."

"But, Nassir, you didn't show it," I gasped. "We never knew, never dreamed—why you must be joking, or it's just something that happened in your mind after the shock of Conrad's death. I know how that can be. I almost lost my head too, but-"

"No," Nassir said firmly. "This started long, long before that. From the time I came back with Conrad, or maybe even before that, when he talked about you and read me parts of your letters. How bitterly I envied him. The bitterness went away gradually, during the years we all worked together and became such close friends. I went on loving you, but I knew it was something that would never harm you or Conrad, something you'd never even know about."

I looked up, and Nassir's clean eyes met mine honestly. His face blurred to me. I leaned my cheek against his hand that still held mine tightly.

"I'm sorry, Nassir," I whispered. "But thank you for telling me."

A nurse came toward us, smiling. "Your aunt would like to see you," she said.

Nassir and I went in together.

Aunt Myrna smiled at us drowsily. "I'm all right," she said. "I knew I would be, after you came home, Abena." She looked at Nassir. "You're a good boy," she said. "As good as our Conrad. You found Abena for me again. I'll always be grateful for that."

I lived with Aunt Myrna and nursed her back to health myself those summer months that followed. And while Aunt Myrna's body healed, so did my soul. With the coming of another fall season, I felt whole again. The grief and the pain subsided because there was a difference. I was not alone. I had two people who loved me.

I was busy planting chrysanthemums in the garden one afternoon when Nassir walked toward me through the garden. "I thought you might be able to use this," he said. He was carrying a sundial. I touched the carved words on its pedestal with my fingers:

HOURS PASS, FLEET DAYS AND YEARS; ONLY LOVE STAYS

The smile that came to Nassir's face was a wonderful thing to see. Healing comes when you let the heart love again. I knew it was the beginning of a wonderful new love for me.

THE END

PLAYER FOR LIFE
I used men for sex to protect my heart

"**P**aul, I'm serious. There's nothing to discuss." I fought to control the anger within me as I slammed the door on my boyfriend's brand new Honda Prelude. I couldn't believe he'd just taken me to such an elaborate restaurant simply to celebrate buying a new car.

"But Jackie it's not just your ordinary car!" he had bragged. Paul was an enterprising MBA graduate who specialized in those trendy new electronic tax-filing businesses. He thought too highly of his financial accomplishments though I'd loved him deeply. "Listen, didn't I tell you I custom ordered dual CD and cassette players, as well as…"

And on and on he'd jabbered as if the darned thing had wings. When he'd called me earlier in the day for a "special evening," my hopes had soared. Maybe this would be the night he proposed, I'd thought. Instead, as we ate desert I'd steered our conversation to us being more specific about our future, and he flipped. It had been as though I'd never known the man.

Now, as I rushed to the door of my condo, I realized how true that was.

"Hey Jackie, what is this?" Paul caught up with me halfway up the walkway. "Will you please wait? I didn't say I never wanted to get married. I simply said…I said I wasn't ready for marriage at this time. Hell, we're both twenty-six. There's plenty of time."

I held out the "stop" sign with my palms. "Forget it Paul. What you're actually saying is you don't want to marry me. That's it, isn't it? Successful brother like you is bound to marry someday soon. It's right for the image. But after three long years of practically living together, you simply don't love me enough to make me that special someone."

We both stood there staring at each other. I expected a rebuttal from him. When no reply came, I sadly concluded my comment had hit the mark. Paul hadn't loved me after all. My stomach became violently ill as I turned and hurried inside.

I slammed the door but didn't turn on any lights. My heart joined my stomach! I simply leaned against the door. As his new car sped, away I silently said good-bye and then burst into full-blown tears.

For two whole days I cried almost non-stop. He didn't call and I missed him terribly. When he had said that we both should keep our own living place rather than move in together, I had only slightly questioned his love. When some friends of mine had caught him at a

37

club smooching up to another woman, I had accused them of trying to split us apart. And after I myself had caught the smooth rascal in one cheating lie after another, I simply thought he needed to grow up. "Boys will always be boys," I'd said. Oh, how wrong I'd been.

Still, for almost an entire week, I expected Paul to ring my phone. If nothing else, my female pride assured me he'd come back for some more good loving. That man could lay it down heavy, and I knew how much he adored my willing body. I was even determined to really "put it on him" when he returned. However, the only person who interrupted my thoughts over the next few days was my dear friend Kim.

"Now that's what I call actually kicking a man to the curb!" Kim exclaimed over the phone after I told her how I jumped out of Paul's car. She was merely teasing, though. She knew the depths of my love for Paul and how down I'd been.

"It's nothing more than that scoundrel deserves. Girl, you know Bernice and I tried to tell you way back when-"

"Yeah, yeah, I know." I didn't want to be reminded. "Anyway, what's new at the office. I'll be in tomorrow. Three days is long enough to mourn the likes of that man."

"Uh-huh! Especially since tomorrow is payday." We both laughed before she took on that gossipy tone of voice. "But ooooh child, wait till you see what's down the hall from you now. Girl I swear, this man can melt butter just by looking at it."

"Kim! Kim! Are you crazy? I just broke up with Paul. The last thing I'm looking for is another relationship," I huffed into the phone. "I just broke up with my man, I'm really not interested in someone else!"

"True dat! But you said yourself it's time to move one," she sighed. Nonetheless, she proceeded to give me the 411 on some new accountant named Marvin. The name sounded sort of weak, however, it was my knees that went wobbly the very next day when I feasted upon this handsome brother.

I worked as a junior merger specialist in the main headquarters of one of the largest banks on the West Coast. Our huge San Francisco office spurned relationships that led to many romances and even marriages. But soon after I was introduced to handsome Marvin Young, the office rumors rattled. In fact, the night before Kim had already started trying to get me to go after Marvin. But there was no way I was going to let another man in my heart.

Thus the next day I was greeted with "Girl, I'm telling you what I know. You really need to get with this brother," Kim rambled on. "He just might be what you need to get over Paul. I heard Marvin's a player though." I rolled my eyes in my head. My friend was trying to hook me up with another dog!

Twenty-eight year old Marvin was about as tall as Michael Jordan and kept his head shaved clean like the former basketball star. He even waltzed around the office halls with pure, athletic grace. He was simply too attractive and apparently stuck on himself. His physique appeared firm and ready for either bedroom or boardroom action. According to the rumors, he seemed to be doing impressive work in both places.

Marvin had been assigned to do some sharp-shooting work at a few of the branch offices throughout the country. No one particularly wanted to do that much traveling but his position centered around a special project for one of the vice-presidents. So it had become a hot, plum assignment. He quickly became the envy and admiration of us young, upward mobile executives.

Likewise, with just as much speed, Marvin moved in on probably the most eligible female in the entire building. She had a prestigious loan job, she held a MBA, and her family was wealthy. Furthermore, she was drop-dead gorgeous and she knew it. This brother really got around.

Through our brief encounters Marvin did seem to match up to his scandalous reputation. I was outwardly cool toward him. Besides, I was still getting over my grief. I still believed that someday soon Paul would call to patch up things. Sadly, that call never came, not even once. It was like we had never existed. Somewhere during this time my heart turned real cold. I started to use men to my advantage, the way I had been used. My bedroom was like a train station and I didn't care. As long as my sexual desires were being fulfilled, I could forget about how much love had torn my once fragile heart.

It didn't take that much to convince me to be a player because only a year earlier a two-timing husband had dumped my older sister. Before that, my mom had struggled without a man to raise us. As a young, impressionable girl, I believed it had been my father's fault my mom had it so hard. To me, it seemed men were nothing but trouble. The least I could do was use men the way they had always used women.

Thus when I finally did sit down with Marvin Young, my attitude reflected, "What's love got to do with it?" Right then all I wanted to do was establish my career. I was still a very passionate person and to quench this desire for intimacy I decided to limit myself to an occasional fling now and then. If the fling lasted only one night, so what? There were more where that came from. Wasn't that the way dogish men handled women?

"I notice you put in quite late hours around here too," Marvin said to me, as he stuck his smiling face into my office early one evening. He had been with the bank for about three months now, and we had bumped into each other like this because we both worked in the same general area.

"Tell me about it!" I replied wearily. "I see you're at it again too."

As Marvin stepped even closer inside my space, his cologne pleased my nostrils. I inhaled like I'd been suffocating for air. I also attempted not to savor how delicious his full lips looked. And the magic in his eyes were music to my hungry soul.

Though I had displayed an outward mentality of live and let live, I remembered the deep, romantic bond of I once had with Paul. Nonethelss, I had enjoyed using men for sensual satisfaction only. Being a player had some rewards. So my entire sensuality was on full alert as Marvin stood in front of my desk.

"I guess if we keep meeting like this the rumor mill will crank up on us," he said lightly. "And I suppose if I ask you out to dinner then we'll start a verbal circus."

Inside, my heart lunged! Outwardly I was cool. "Well now that depends on if I were to accept. Are you seriously asking?"

He leaned over so close I knew he could hear my erratic breathing. "I'm always serious. Haven't you heard?"

"Uh-huh. Which reminds me of something else I've heard. There's a certain Ms. Mobley who might not just gossip about us. I heard you're sleeping with her. She would start an all out, fever-pitch claim to you."

Marvin smiled but he didn't miss a beat. "Please! I thought you were sharper than that Jackie. Surely, you've observed how Joyce and I are merely acquaintances. Close maybe, but still…"

He was right. I had noticed a certain cooling off with them two. More accurately, the rumor mill gossiped that Marvin's womanizing ways were back in full stride. I'd heard of and had seen him whispering closely in a couple of female ears. I thought of my lonely nights and my "just use em" attitude. Maybe Marvin could help me out in my time of need. My hesitance disappeared. I became bold and assertive.

"If you're sure I'm not stepping on anyone's toes."

"I'm sure." To my satisfaction Marvin did sound sincerely anxious. There was a fresh, manly look about him that didn't match the "player" category the girls put him into. I shrugged it off to sexual desires. Marvin simply wanted my body and knew the correct face he had to maintain. But boy, if he only realized how badly I wanted him to possess my body.

Anyway, over the course of the next few weeks, Marvin and I had several after-work dinners and a few lunches. I found myself making excuses to work late. For one, I didn't want to be at home if and when Paul called. The other reason I worked late was to be around the only person who was paying me the type of attention I craved.

During our outings, we didn't call them official dates, I learned a lot about Marvin. He made me laugh while at the same time he was thought provoking and had a keen business sense. The man even had a mental map for where he wanted to go in life. It was a growing treat to be around Mr. Young.

"I can imagine the rumors have really started about us now," Marvin commented one night a quaint bar. We were waiting on a table at the popular restaurant. "Have they got us married yet?"

"Nope," I answered. It was the truth. I knew Marvin probably dated others but I didn't care. "They know me and they think they know you."

He arched his eyebrow. Marvin was always a lively person; however, my comment seemed to perk him up even more. "Oh? Well I'm definitely curious to hear what the ladies have to say about me. But right now I'm more interested in learning all I can about you Jackie. You say they think they know you? Please. Do tell."

I should have shut my bold big mouth up. Remembering my new outlook toward relationships, I chose my words carefully. "Marvin, I was recently with a guy who hurt me terribly."

"You wanted one thing and he wanted another."

"Exactly! Have you been listening to the rumors or talked—"

"No. Most relationships fail because of the same principle-lack of true communication." Marvin signaled the bartender for a refill of our drinks. "That's what makes this little conversation so much more interesting. I think it will lead us to discussing directions."

"Directions?" I picked up my drink. "I think you better give me some because I'm lost as to what you're talking about."

He scooted closer. "We'll get back to that in a sec. First, back to this clown who dumped you."

"Whoa there Mister! Who said he dumped me? Maybe I kicked him to the curb."

"Perhaps. It doesn't really matter. What matters is he dissed the way you felt about the relationship. Otherwise there still would be a relationship." The perception of his mind caused me to glow inside. "You see, that's direction. Now you let it be known that you're not looking to fall in love, maybe a little company once in awhile to keep the bed warm. Is that what the girls know about you, dear Jackie?"

My eyes blinked once too often. I almost couldn't believe my ears. Surely he had talked with or overheard Kim and Bernice talking. But then again, I hadn't openly expressed my outlook to anyone. It was more in the lifestyle I led.

When I didn't verbally respond, rather just watched him as I sipped my drink, Marvin continued low and slow. "What you're telling me is you're a lady trying to steer clear of love for now. You don't intend to be hurt anymore."

41

My word! Of course I couldn't admit that, so I disguised the truth with a modern, professional, working-girl answer. "Not really Marv. Let's just say I want to establish my career before settling down. It's enough of a hassle staying ahead of the rat race. Who has time for love, right?"

He looked at me as though he hadn't believed a word I'd said. "What's love got to do with it?" After he said that I intuitively knew where our evening would end. This suave man was reading my soul so well; it was like he lived inside my head. I simply tilted my now empty glass to him.

"Are you telling me that's the way the ladies have me pegged too?" His face was right next to mine. "Is that how you see me Jackie?"

Just then our names were announced for the next available table. Marvin paid our bar tab. As he led us out of the lounge, my legs were a little shaky; the alcohol combined with the deep conversation had me spinning. And to dazzle me even further Marvin walked us not to the adjacent restaurant, but headed toward the door.

"I'm hungry as a horse!" he said to my amusement before leading the way outside.

"Then why are we…"

"For you dear lady. I'm hungry for you." Out on the sidewalk he leaned down to kiss me briefly for the first time. That initial contact zoomed my passionate arousal clear to my toes. I was prepared to beg for more when he moved from me and flashed a wicked smile.

"I like you a lot Jackie. We both like each other, it's obvious. But whereas you may be just pretending, I'm for real about not looking for a serious relationship right now." He traced a single finger across my still trembling lips. "How about it? You game for a little intimacy without all the strings attached?"

I exhaled deeply. "I'm not looking for any obligations Marvin."

"So…we can…"

"Your place or mine?" I heard my steady, brave voice whisper.

We chose his place. And once inside Marvin's bedroom, I became braver still. I mean, I was never inhibited while making love to someone I cared about. However, here I was with a new guy, a new attitude, and apparently a new sex drive. I don't know, maybe it was the alcohol that fueled me. Maybe deep inside I actually liked Marvin more than I had admitted. Or perhaps it was because my body had been deprived for far too long. Whatever, I knew I wanted to greedily conquer and be conquered.

Gradually though, I discovered more than anything else, my lustful spirit was on fire because of the masterful way Marvin danced earth shattering delight on my body. After elegantly undressing me to complete nudity, he teased me with patience. He removed his shirt to display a chiseled upper body. My heart fluttered! My hungry hands explored his tight, gorgeous flesh. Marvin prolonged the ecstasy by teasing with me half-dressed. We kissed and rolled over his king-sized bed like two hormone-driven college students. My thirsty tongue could not get enough of his delicious, sweet tasting mouth.

Then he placed my hands upon his shoulders. Although, what I really wanted to do was rip off his pants. Yet my new lover was in charge as he played angelic music over my hardened nipples with his skilled tongue. How sweet and warm my breast felt nestled within his lips. Breathing normally was out of the question. My chest felt like it was going to explode.

"Oh please, please!" I somehow begged.

"But you're…so lovely," he whispered. "I simply want to enjoy more of your beauty first."

Those wonderful words had to have come from heaven! How could I deny him? Indeed, Marvin's eyes shimmered over me with the intensity of a beggar searching for gold. He gently, yet forcefully, squeezed every erotic drop of rapture from my core before finally removing his pants and slowly joining our bodies together as one. By then I had squirmed and screamed mercifully. When his deep love strokes became demandingly long and full, my joy spilled out in one glorious crescendo.

Afterwards I continued to roam my hands and mouth over his hairy, moist flesh. I knew my female behavior was being possessive but I couldn't help myself. This player had satisfied me totally.

"A gal could get used to this Mr. Young," I purred. My desire was rekindling that quickly.

Marvin turned on his side to face me. He leaned over to kiss my inquisitive hands. "Not you. Certainly a sassy, classy lady with your attitude doesn't want to get used to this. Why, that would mean some type of commitment, wouldn't it?"

His words were a bit accusing. But I played it cool. Instead of being all lovey dovey, I switched roles. Grabbing a hold of his fresh hardness, I aggressively straddled him and became more of the sexy, free-spirited woman I knew he preferred.

And that was the way we played it every time we came together after that. We saw each other once or twice a week even though I wanted more. Occasionally, I'd seen him leaving the building with another female co-worker. Whenever I found the nerve to question him, he said it was nothing and further reminded me of our "directions", which we had mapped out so clearly.

So I bit my tongue and went right along in that direction. What else could I do? Marvin not only saturated me physically; he was so

43

mentally stimulating as well. He was more than any woman could ask for. That's what made my hard-core pretense so frustrating. Following the breakup with Paul I really had adopted a female "player" attitude. I used men the same way their doggish behinds played women. Yet who knew that I'd meet someone like Marvin so soon. And who said he wouldn't show those same reversible stripes in due time. As it was already, he seemed back and forth with his emotions towards me. At times he appeared as though he couldn't get enough of our being together. Then at other times he acted like he cared less than two cents for me.

All I knew was that my growing affection for him had me wanting to declare a "change in directions". I was falling in love. On the other hand I truly didn't want to be in love with such a playboy.

"Then why don't you lay it on the line to him!" Kim almost shouted in my ear one day while we were out shopping. "You're making good money and he's making megabucks. Girl get that man to stay put or somebody else will. You know he's getting ready to take all those trips to the branch offices."

"Don't remind me. There might be weeks when we won't see each other. But Kim, I can't just change boats in the middle of the stream. We decided early how things would be. I went into this with my eyes wide-open. Besides, I admire that about him. If Paul and I had of done the same maybe I wouldn't have wasted three years."

Kim sighed, probably feeling my predicament. "Yeah, well something must be going on because that other player in our office, Mike, the last brother you slept with, wanted to know why you've been avoiding him."

"What! The dog of all dogs?"

"Yes," she exclaimed, as we left the mall and headed toward the food court. "And if I recall, you didn't think he was so bad a few months ago."

Inwardly I cringed at the thought that Mike had been one of my flings during my current "player" days. Now the only person I cared to play with was Marvin.

"Now get this! Mike claims it was Marvin himself who told him you were fair game. He says Marvin said you two were only friends."

That hurt was so painful I was glad my friend couldn't see my moist eyes in the shopping crowd. I couldn't believe Marvin had said such a thing but I knew he probably had. It all served to remind me of my attitude toward men in general. I never should've allowed my heart to fall in love again. At least not falling so far whereas I couldn't pull myself out. And if that's the game Marvin was truly playing, well then I was going to revert back to my funky, cold attitude too.

A small team was assembled to travel with Marvin to several

locations. Since I too worked in acquisitions and mergers, my boss informed me it would be a good idea if I joined up with the group in San Antonio.

Before the trip, though, this old fling, Mike Washington, attempted to rekindle the physical bedroom activities we had enacted in the past. Since Marvin had told him we were simply friends, I went out with him merely to get back at Marvin. But my heart wasn't in it any longer. I didn't want to experience the obvious hurt that was coming because Marvin didn't love me, as I loved him. I concluded that maybe someday, when I'm over the hurt of Marvin, I'd get back my old attitude. But for now, I had to go through all the changes with him.

"What's this foolishness with Mike?" Marvin questioned as I stood at the check-in counter of the downtown San Antonio Hilton. I'd just gotten in from the airport and was quite surprised with his remarks. He had heard about my recent fling with Mike. It seemed I had made him jealous. That was the reason why I'd gone out with Mike in the first place.

"My goodness Marvin, it's good to see you too!" The desk clerk quickly handed me my keys. I then turned and gave my suitcase to Marvin. He had to hurry to keep up with my long stride as I practically ran down the hallway.

"Now isn't it amazing what one can hear all the way out here in Texas!" I continued. We joined three other people already waiting on the elevator so I lowered my voice. I leaned in closer for a sniff of Marvin's delightful cologne. "You were so cool and laid back at home, never seeming to care who I dated."

When the elevator stopped we remained quiet. I enjoyed his slight anxiety though I wasn't sure what to make of it. Was he jealous now simply because he knew someone else was sleeping with me? Or had he experienced a change of "directions" in his heart?

Finally we were the only ones left in the elevators as we headed to the tenth floor. We turned to face each other and I knew he'd missed me too. Our lips were like magnets. Our tongues glided over the others' in one delicious reunion of joy. My heart leaped in my chest. I was deep in love and there was nothing I could do about it.

I pulled myself from his kiss, remembering how he questioned me. "From what Mike tells me, you were the one who told him we were mere bed partners," I snapped.

He exhaled in apparent frustration. "Just forget him, okay? Let's just get you settled in and forget I even brought up the name."

Well, so much for his change of heart. It looked as though he still didn't care whom I went out with. Maybe I should've stayed with Mike, put it in the rumor mill, and see how that grabbed him.

In any event, I became dead serious about knowing where I stood in his life. Marvin wanted it his way so he could be free to date others. At the same time he didn't like that direction when it seemed I too, played the same course. Who needed such a hassle? Though it might have taken a while, I would get Marvin out of my system even if it meant inviting a whole slew of men to my bed.

I was prepared to confront Marvin as soon as I could.

I received a phone call from the wet coast the next day. My boss wanted further explanation of a report I'd left behind. While on the phone she asked me how the trip was going so far.

"I can see some usefulness in this venture," I spoke hesitantly. "This morning we discussed some local matters at the main branch here. But you know it's not much of a merger-type expedition. Everyone is so concerned about Marvin Young and his crew of accountants combing through their books. "

"Hmm. We figured as much. Still it was Marvin who insisted on having you along." I knew this elder lady was not part of the notorious grapevine. She was speaking the gospel truth. She went on to say how persistent Marvin had been about me being on this trip.

My thoughts were jumbled in my head. The only time we had discussed the trip was when I had brought it up. Why hadn't he volunteered his input then? And just why did he want me along anyway? To keep me away from Mike or because he really cared and wanted me close? Surely if he were such a "player" this would have been the perfect opportunity for him to have a little fun on the side.

Later that evening we went out with one of Marvin's college buddies. I kept checking his emotions out of the corner of my eye. One minute I felt he truly loved me and was simply afraid to admit it. The next second I was just as sure he was like all the other men I'd gone out with. He wanted his cake with all the trimmings regardless of my feelings.

As we sat at an outdoors restaurant on the scenic waterfront of downtown San Antonio, my curiosity had driven me crazy inside. Suddenly, Marvin excused himself to the restroom.

"Listen Jackie, I know my friend Marvin puts up this casual front like he doesn't really care but believe me, I know the man. You are real special to him. He hasn't stopped talking about you," His friend Frank said.

"You don't have to score points for him. We already have this understanding. Our relationship."

"What? That directions crap? Woman, can't you see that's just to protect his heart? He was devastated by someone he loved." I looked at Frank in disbelief. "Some no good for nothing…anyway she didn't return his love. A brother like that with so much to offer and she broke his heart."

"She broke it off?"

"No, he did. After he found out she had been openly cheating on him. And that's when he came up with that directions stuff. He swore he'd never fall in love again unless it was on his own terms." We both looked up and saw Marvin returning. His friend rushed on, "But you're different Jackie. I can tell you're melting his heart so don't let him get away."

And as Marvin approached I saw him clearly for what he was. It was like looking at a male image of myself. Who said a man's heart couldn't be wounded like a woman's? Marvin had been hurt and had adapted the same self-protection for himself as I had. We were just alike and I intended to set him straight about it too.

The next morning, I thought I'd see just how much Marvin wanted me to stay there in Texas. I pretended to be leaving, hoping he would ask me to stay.

"Where do you think you're going? There are plenty of meetings left to this trip-" he said.

"Marvin I have work to do back at the office. And if I remember correctly, Mike was going to get two tickets for a concert in Oakland tonight," I lied to Marvin about my so-called departure. "If I catch the nine o'clock flight, the jet lag won't be so bad later this evening."

I sure hoped my brain knew what it was doing. I had called his room as he was waking up. I held the laughter in my chest. My empty suitcase was "packed" right by the door.

"But...Jackie, baby look."

"No, you look. Baby!" Though I sincerely sympathized with his reasons, I was in no mood for my heart to be played like he was doing. We had both been hurt by our pasts. But I had learned life was too short for the games he and I were playing.

"Now you know good and well I don't enjoy sleeping around like the rumors make me out to be," I continued sharply.

"Rumors?" he questioned. "Are you saying that before we became involved you didn't live sort of loose?"

I smiled with slight embarrassment. "Sort of, yes. But that was only to protect my heart. I told you how badly I'd been hurt Paul."

"So you slept with Tom, Dick and Harry to make up for the lost time you put in with this other guy?"

."No Marvin, it had more to do with self-preservation. I acted that way...behaved that way so guys would see me differently. I didn't want anyone to take me seriously. The hurt was too deep, so I thought I'd saved men the "I love you' speech."

"So if they knew you didn't love them, there would be no obligation on their part to say they loved you, especially when they could have sex without it? Well, why didn't you say all this when we first started out? Why didn't you say you were falling in love with me?"

"I said what I thought you wanted to hear. And don't act like you didn't tell me the same Marvin!"

"Uh-huh. But what I don't understand is why you're changing directions now? What makes you think anything is different with me? I told you how I felt—"

"I only thought, that, like me, you've been...Look! To hell with all of this! I'm outta here!" I shouted. "Unless you have one good reason for me to stay. No. Make that two good reasons."

He frowned like a little boy. "Like I love you? Jackie, you know I do."

My heart jumped but I remained "And reason number two?"

Now Marvin really sounded puzzled. "Marriage Jackie. I admit I might've been fronting with this loose, cool attitude, but I love you. I think we should become exclusive. I've seen how people change just when you're certain you know how they feel, but I want to give this another chance."

I knew what he meant. He was afraid of the same thing I was. I thought I'd known Paul. "No, marriage isn't necessary, at least not yet. A long-term commitment will do for now. Don't you see, we've both have our reasons for shielding our hearts. But this is the only way we can find true love again. I'm willing to take a chance. I don't wanna be a player anymore."

"Sounds like a record," he smiled. "Okay, okay, I'm willing to try if you are."

"And listen, no fooling around Mr. Young. You had better be a one-woman man."

"Me? You're the one everybody needed a score card to keep up with."

"And I thought you didn't listen to the rumor mill chit-chat," I said, laughing in his ear.

Marvin instantly caught onto the joke. "Why you faker! That suitcase isn't really packed is it? What would you have done if I hadn't fallen for your phony plot."

"Oh but you did! Hang up Marvin," I harped before leaving my room and coming to his. Then I sashayed from him toward the bed. "You want to see another surprise?"

I slowly unfastened my London Fog coat to reveal how undressed I was underneath. My sensuous juices flowed heavy as Marvin's eyes went all lusty over my skimpy, red bra and panties.

From them on we were like two people who had been in prison for centuries. Our true emotions had been locked away behind a barricade of false emotions. Now, however, we had let the full range of our true love for each other come steaming out.

Marvin made love to me like he'd always done. It was the spirit

48

of his soul that was different this time. I could taste how much he was letting go of leashed up emotions. And of course I responded by letting my guard down. He touched my life that much more because I knew it wasn't about a physical thing. We shared love from the depths of our existence, as real people, not as players.

It was truly a blessing that Marvin's friend confided in me as he'd done. I'm not sure how we would have turned out if he hadn't. I sensed somewhere deep within himself that Marvin did honestly love me. I often wonder how many men and women out there who seem to be "players" are actually people who've been hurt, or have seen the devastation of unrequited love, and as a result have limited their affections to only physical intimacy. Thank heavens I discovered the difference before I threw love away.

THE END

BROKEN SEX PROMISES
I'd Love Him But He Won't Let Me

I knew Chad was a fine man, and he would make some woman very happy. And even though I'd dated him for two months, I knew that woman wasn't me. Sure, I enjoyed the fancy places he took me to. The delicious meals we shared were nice, too. But the spark—the one that's rare and illusive—just wasn't there. When he touched me or kissed me, it was nice and could even be described as pleasant. But that was it, end of sentence. Could I really commit myself to a man who didn't get my blood pumping and my motor racing? I didn't think so.

I knew the reason for my hesitancy concerning Chad. Though I cared for him, he still wasn't Tony.

Just thinking of my ex-lover caused my heart to quicken and my body to tingle. With amazing clarity, I remembered how it felt when his strong, brown fingers stroked and caressed my heated skin. I recalled how his dark, heavy-lidded eyes had raked over me. Without the benefit of words, his expression openly spoke of how much he wanted me. And the feeling was mutual. Tony had ruined me for other men, and I wondered if I would ever get over him.

Tony Markell was the kind of man that you didn't take home to mama. He was gorgeous, sexy, and way too smooth. When mothers saw him coming, they shielded their daughter's eyes and rushed them away to the safe shelter of their own homes.

Females had an intuition about guys like Tony. He was just so hot that there was no way to prevent the fatal burns that a relationship with him could and would produce. He had left a trail of victims with broken hearts behind, and everyone assumed more would follow.

I guess that's why I was so surprised by my own attraction to Tony. Normally, I fell for the stable, responsible type of man who would treat me right and respect me. Of course, that type usually provided no excitement and hardly any thrills.

But Tony was a whole other type of man. Though I tried to resist him, he had me back at my place and out of my clothes by our third date. Something told me that he usually worked much quicker, but he was being patient with me.

"I've wanted you all night," he murmured, his lips doing magical things along the column of my neck. He took a short detour down my bare shoulder sending a jolt of electric thrills straight to my private, womanly places.

My fingers danced along the tightly corded muscles of his back. "I want you too, Tony," I whispered, still not believing that I was with the man of my dreams—or of my nightmares, depending on which way I examined it.

He brought his mouth lower, his warm tongue grazing my swollen nipple. He sucked hard, and I nearly melted on the spot.

I was no stranger to men, but I was a novice when it came to the types of feelings that Tony was producing in me. Every nerve cell in my passion-starved body was crying out for the ecstasy that this man could offer. And once our hungry bodies came together in the ultimate explosion of harmonious loving, I knew I would never be the same.

That experience with Tony changed me, all right. It left me flying high into the clouds, and then almost immediately, crashed me back to reality.

"I really enjoyed last night, Tony," I said, cradling the phone between my neck and my shoulder. Though he hadn't spent the entire night in my bed, we had spent a good portion of it making love. I could hardly wait for dawn to break so I could call him and hear his sweet voice.

"Yeah, well, I had a good time too, Marissa," he replied, his cool tone in sharp contrast to the hot way he had spoken to me the night before.

"Can we get together tonight?" I asked, hoping that maybe I had misinterpreted his voice. Maybe he was still tired or was just missing me, too.

"You know, Marissa, I've been thinking…" His voice trailed off and something told me that whatever he had to say, I wasn't going to like it.

"What is it, Tony?" I absently twirled a strand of my hair, trying to quell my inner nervousness.

"We've been moving a little fast. Maybe a little too fast, if you know what I mean."

"No, I don't think I know what you mean," I replied tartly, my feelings hurt and my pride wounded.

"I'm just saying that perhaps we should back off a little bit and think about things. Let's not get all clingy with each other. Okay?"

My mouth dropped open and my heart dropped to my feet. When I slept with Tony, I had given him a piece of myself, and now, he was thrusting it back in my face. My gift of love was being returned now that it had been unwrapped and used. I felt like a fool.

"You're a real jerk!" I hissed, covering my pain with anger. It was either get mad or start crying, and I wasn't gonna give him the satisfaction of my tears.

"Come on, baby. Don't be like this. We had a good time. Are you going to go and get all possessive on me?"

I wished we were in the same room so I could show him just how possessive I felt. I would have shoved his sorry butt to the curb.

"Marissa, I was thinking. Maybe when my life slows down a little, we can get together again. A re-creation of last night would be fun." His voice took on a husky, flirty tone.

"I don't think so," I replied lightly, shoving my hurt down and pretending that he didn't matter to me. I knew that later, when I was all alone, I would allow myself the luxury of a good cry.

I didn't see Tony for several months. By the time I did run in to him, I was already involved with Chad.

I knew what had happened was for the best. It was better that I had been dumped sooner rather than later. Now that I was with Chad, I wouldn't have to worry about getting my heart broken. Chad made it clear that he was a one-woman man and that he was looking for some permanency in his life.

"I want to settle down and have kids," he said, his dark, piercing eyes so sincere.

I gnawed on my lip wondering just what constituted an appropriate response in this circumstance. I cared for the man, but marriage had never crossed my mind. Then again, maybe I was jumping to conclusions. Chad never actually proposed to me. Perhaps I was only assuming that he was talking about me.

"Marissa, you have come to mean so much to me." Chad took my hand and gently kissed my palm. "I can only hope that you feel the same way about me."

I swallowed the lump in my throat and licked my suddenly dry lips. We were moving much too fast, and I knew that I would have to put the breaks on our growing relationship. I didn't have a choice. Running into Tony has proved to me that I couldn't give myself to Chad. Not when my heart still belonged to my ex-lover.

"Girl, are you ill or are you just crazy?" my friend Nikki asked when I told her I was thinking of breaking it off with Chad. She put her hand on my forehead and pretended to take my temperature.

I slapped her hand away and touched the center of my chest. "My problem isn't up there, but it's in here."

Nikki shook her head. "Honey, you better explain yourself because nothing you're talking about is making any sense."

"Can't you understand that Chad doesn't get my heart pounding or my juices flowing?" I slumped down in my chair, feeling miserable.

Nikki snapped her fingers. "Oh, I get it now. You're comparing Chad to that no good, cheating lounge singer."

I jumped to my feet, somehow feeling the need to defend the one man who had hurt me. "He is not a lounge singer," I argued. "He's a musician."

52

Nikki rolled her eyes. "Whatever. He could be the artist formerly known as Prince, and he still couldn't hold a candle to Chad. Now there's one fine looking brother—and he's a lawyer, too!" She got all dreamy-eyed and I had to wonder if maybe she had a crush on my soon-to-be ex-boyfriend.

"Money isn't everything, you know." I picked at some loose fingernail polish and avoided her eyes.

"No, it isn't, but it sure is up there with the top three." A slight smile curled her lips upward. "Aw, come on, Marissa. Let me live vicariously through you. Chad's a great guy."

A sly grin of my own lit up my face. "That may be so, but Tony was so hot in bed that I'm surprised I didn't spontaneously combust. I feel like he left me branded with his initials in my very soul."

"Mmm hmm, you and hundreds of other girls feel the exact same way about the man. I hope you had the smarts to practice safe sex. There's no telling where his thang's been." She cackled with laughter at what she thought was a funny joke. I wasn't amused.

"Very funny-not!"

Though my best friend's ribbing did tick me off, it did give me something to think about. Tony had dated me three times, taken me to bed, and then promptly dumped me. He was a woman crusher who only thought about himself.

But Chad was patient with me. He was kind and caring, and he put no pressure on me to move forward in a physical sense. We had kissed and even made out a little, but when I pulled back, he didn't push the issue. He told me that he wanted me, but he was willing to wait until I was ready to move forward to the next level.

Though I was grateful that he didn't try to rush me into bed, a part of me did wish that he was more forceful. Maybe if he were to pull me against him and thrust his tongue into my mouth, I would feel something other than polite friendship for the man.

Despite my misgivings, I didn't break it off with Chad. I did care about him, and I did enjoy the times we spent together. I thought I was hoping against all odds that the missing catalyst that we needed to spark a little passion in our fairly sedate relationship would magically appear. And it might have worked—except for one thing. I saw Tony again.

Nikki and I were in a popular nightclub, needing a little girl's night put. This place was rumored to have the best music in town, and on Thursdays, drinks for women were half price. With a deal like that, Nikki and I planned on having a good time. We were going to stay out late and party till we dropped. And that would have happened if I hadn't received an unexpected and totally unwanted surprise.

The man who had caused me such inner turmoil was standing in front of me. He looked even more handsome, and his smile was just as wide and charming.

"Marissa, baby, aren't you a sight for sore eyes." His gaze slid over my body, igniting a fire that hadn't been lit in months. I resented the way this man made me feel, and I determined that I wouldn't let him see the effect that he had on me. I tamped down on my emotions and met his stare head on.

"Tony," I said, attempting to sound indifferent. "If I had known it was your band playing here tonight, I would have gone elsewhere."

He tipped his head upward and laughed. "Ah, Marissa, you wound my heart."

"Oh, I doubt that. In order for that to happen, you'd have to have a heart."

A single eyebrow quirked upward. "I see the lady's still angry. You should really get over that. It'll only make you bitter and old."

I glared at him and downed my drink in one long gulp. If I had to drink a dozen others just to clear my head of Tony, I would.

He made a disapproving sound with his tongue and grabbed me by the arm. Against my protests, he pulled me out of my seat and led me to a private corner at the back of the bar.

"Let go of me," I demanded, pulling against his hand. It was useless. He had me in a steel grip and wasn't letting go.

"Chill out, woman. We need to talk." He grabbed my other hand and backed me up against the wall.

"You know, I could scream and get you into a whole lot of trouble."

Tony just chuckled and brought his lips to my ear. His hot breath sent a sizzling arrow straight through me.

"Calm down, baby. I just wanted to have a private talk with you. There's no law against that, is there?"

I opened my mouth to issue a sharp retort but closed it just as fast. I knew there was no use arguing with Tony. He would have his say. The sooner I settled down and listened, the sooner I could get back to my table and commence drowning my sorrows.

"Fine, speak your mind and then go away. I've got better things to do with my time."

He dropped my hands and took a very small step backwards. Though he'd put about a half-foot distance between the two of us, it wasn't nearly enough. I could still feel his breath on my face and the heat from his body caused a liquid warmth to settle over me.

Tony wet his lips and ran his fingers through my hair. I would have backed away if it wasn't for the fact that I was standing against the wall. But then again, I couldn't kid myself. Having Tony's hands on me felt wonderful, and though I should have pushed him away, I didn't.

"I've missed you, Marissa," he whispered.

His fingertips roamed down to the back of my neck causing a tiny sigh to escape from my parted lips. My mind advised me to flee. My traitorous body begged me to stay. In a split-second decision, my heated flesh won the battle, and I found myself leaning in to Tony's touch.

"You don't know how much I wanted to see you and to call you," he murmured, his lips so temptingly close to mine.

"Why didn't you?" I asked, a slight amount of accusation peppering my words.

Tony didn't answer. Instead, he lowered his mouth to mine in a kiss that halted all rational thought. At the gentle probing of his tongue, I relaxed and allowed him access. There would be no use denying him. I hungered for his touch and his loving. I could no more deny him than I could deny my body food or air. At that moment in time, Tony was my lifeline, and I hung on for dear life.

His hands gripped my waist and brought me flush against the rock hard evidence of his own desire. When he ground against me, I went weak with wanting him. I needed to feel his bare hands against my bare skin, and I would deal with the repercussions later.

"Marissa," he ground out my name, his own lustful state barely concealed. "Honey, I can't leave the bar for another two hours. Please, tell me you'll wait for me."

I was all set to nod in agreement when a voice broke through and shattered the mood.

"Girl, there you are. I've been looking all over for you." Nikki gave Tony such a dirty look that it could have parted the Red Sea. "I need to talk to you."

"Nikki, this isn't a very good time."

"Now!" she said with unaccustomed impatience. "It's very important."

Tony sighed and stepped aside. "Don't go before talking to me, okay?"

Before I could answer, Nikki grabbed me by the hand and pulled me into the restroom. I was beginning to feel like everyone was pushing me around.

"Are you crazy?" she asked the minute the door closed and we were alone. "What are you doing with that woman eater? That guy will devour you up and spit you out again. Is that what you want?"

I folded my arms across my chest and faced her like an angry grizzly bear. "So what if it is? I'm a big girl and I can make my own decisions."

"What if I told you that Chad is out there with a couple of his buddies? Do you still want to go in the back and play bump-and-grind with your old flame?"

My fingers flew to my open mouth. "Oh my god! Are you serious or are you yanking my chain? Is Chad really out there?"

"In the flesh and asking for his best lady." Nikki pulled a paper towel from the dispenser and wet it in the sink. "Here. Your lipstick is smudged. I'll bet half of it's on lover boy's mouth. Serves the dude right."

I did my best to repair my makeup and look presentable. Hopefully, Chad wouldn't notice that my lips were swollen from Tony's love bites or that my eyes were filled with sexual longing for another man.

I walked out of the ladies' room with Nikki and followed her back to our table. By this time, the band had started playing. I recognized the smooth, sultry sound of Tony's voice, and I knew I had to get out of there.

"You can't leave without talking to Chad," Nikki said, pointing to the table where my man was sitting with two of his friends.

When I glanced over to Chad, we made eye contact. He smiled and rose to his feet.

"Hi sweetie. Running in to you is quite a coincidence." He took my hand and brought it to his lips. "Can we join you ladies at your table?"

I shook my head. "Chad, you and I need to talk in private."

I felt miserable, but I knew what I had to do. Now was just as good of time as any. As hard as it would be, I had to be honest with Chad. I wasn't a cheater, but when I kissed Tony, I had betrayed the one man who had been nothing but kind and loving to me. I wouldn't compound the mistake by lying to him about it. I needed to break it off with Chad before I really hurt him.

Chad said good-bye to his friends and took me back to my place. Once there, I spilled it all. I told him that I cared for him, and that I really tried to love him, but my heart already belonged to another.

Chad didn't react at all like I expected. Instead of showing anger or rage, he said he understood.

"I really wanted us to have a future together, Marissa." He leaned back against the couch cushions and let his eyes roam around my sparsely furnished living room. "I even thought we might get married."

I sucked in a deep breath. "I'm so sorry. I didn't mean for any of this to happen."

He wiped a tear from my cheek with the pad of his thumb. "Don't cry. I don't blame you. After all, we can't control our hearts."

"I just don't know what to do," I groaned.

"Well that's simple. Go after him."

"Yeah, right. If I do that, I'll get hurt all over again. I can't trust the man."

Chad shrugged. "If you don't want to do that, you could always marry me. I'd never hurt you or deceive you."

More tears fell down my cheek as I realized what a gem this man was. "You're going to make some lucky woman very happy someday." I kissed him on the cheek and then stood up. "But that woman isn't me. I'm just not good enough for you."

Chad and I said our final good-byes, and I closed that chapter of my life. It was time for me to start a new one.

Unexpectedly and without any warning, Tony showed up at my apartment a few hours later. My eyes were red and swollen from crying and I knew I must have looked awful.

"Go away. I don't want to talk to you." I tried to shut the door, but he blocked it with his foot.

"Too bad because I'm not leaving until you hear me out." He opened the door wider and walked past me. "This conversation is long overdue."

"And whose fault is that?" I huffed.

"Only mine," he said softly. His eyes skimmed over my face. "Do you know how beautiful you are?"

Due to the unexpected compliment, all of the fight left me and I started crying again. It was the last thing I wanted to do, but I couldn't help it. My emotions were raw and I was overcome by my own vulnerability.

"Why did you do what you did, Tony? Why?" I sniffled and fell back onto the couch. He sat down next to me and gripped my fingers between both of his hands.

"I never wanted to, Marissa. You have to believe me."

I squeezed my eyes shut in an attempt to close out the confusing emotions that were running through me. It didn't work. "I don't understand."

Tony reached into his back pocket and pulled out a tiny, tattered photo. It wasn't a normal picture but it was the kind you're given when you have an ultrasound taken. "That's my son."

My head whipped up, astonishment written all over my face. "Your son. Is this some kind of a joke?"

He shook his head and looked down at the picture. "No, it's very real. He's not born yet, but in two short months, I'm going to be a daddy."

"What does this have to do with you and me?" I asked, my voice definitely reaching the freezing point. "You go and make a baby with someone and then you come here to my house?"

"Honey, you have it all wrong. This baby was conceived long before I got involved with you. I only found out about him a few months ago. The morning I broke up with you, to be exact."

I stood to my feet and wrapped my arms around my middle. This was too much. Did I go and lose my heart to Tony only to have him stomp on it again?

"Marissa, don't you see? When my old girlfriend called and told me that she was carrying my baby, I had to break it off with you. I didn't want to, but I knew it was the fair thing to do."

"So, you're back with her now, awaiting your baby's birth?" I fought hard to keep the bitterness at bay.

"That's a laugh. I want nothing to do with Sheena ever again."

I pointed at the picture still in his outstretched fingers. "Isn't that going to be a little difficult since she's the mother of your child?"

"That's what I want to explain. It's been over between Sheena and me for a long time. She only told me about the baby because she didn't intend on keeping it."

"She's giving it up for adoption?"

"No," he insisted. "When my son's born, he's coming home with me. I'm going to raise him."

The wind was knocked out of me as I digested this latest bit of information.

"I know it's unfair to ask this of you," Tony continued, his tone lacking all of the cockiness and self-confidence that I'd come to expect. Instead, he sounded humble and unsure. "But I'd like you to consider raising him with me."

"Are you saying—"

"That I want you to marry me? That's exactly what I'm saying." Tony gripped my shoulders. "I love you, Marissa. I only broke up with you so I could get my life in order. I would have been honest with you from the start, but I was so confused and scared."

Hearing Tony say that something frightened him touched a soft spot in my heart. I still believed that he was wrong, but he was also human.

"Tonight was my last night in the band," he said, his fingers moving in lazy circles on my upper arms. "Next week, I begin managing my uncle's record store."

"Oh, Tony. You love playing in that band. How could you quit?"

"Because I need to be home for my son—and for my wife. Say you'll marry me, Marissa. I promise that you won't regret it."

Of its own accord, the word "yes" dropped from my lips. I brought my hands up to Tony's face and pulled his mouth down to mine in a kiss to seal the deal. It may have been spontaneous and maybe even a little foolhardy, but I knew in my heart that it was right. This was the man I loved, and I would take a chance.

"Are you sure you'll be able to accept my baby as your own?" he asked. His fingers danced down my back and brought my body up against his.

"I'll love him because he's a part of you. Someday, I think we'll even give him a brother or sister. What do you say about that?"

"I say that I'm the happiest man alive!"

Tony picked my up and carried me to my bedroom. After slipping my clothes from my body and removing his own, he placed me on the bed and began renewing his acquaintance with my body. He stroked and kissed and re-ignited the fire that had been smoldering for months. It didn't take much before the embers burst in to red-hot flames.

Tony settled himself between my parted thighs, and eased into the place that was his and his alone. As he brought us to the highest plane of physical love, I knew that my man was home to stay. I was happy and content, and with Tony by my side, it would last forever.

THE END

BEDROOM FANTASIES
I wanted my fiancé's friend

Calvin and I had always been close. For a while we had been inseparable. I couldn't have asked for a better boyfriend. The day he proposed to me had been the greatest day of my life. All I wanted in my world was to be his wife. Being with him was like walking on cloud nine.

That night, he and I were supposed to meet to have dinner. I managed to go through my closet and pick the sexiest thing I could find. When I finally got dressed, Calvin was waiting for me at my door. I rushed to answer it.

"Baby, you're ready! You look nice."

"Well why wouldn't I look nice for my man?" I asked, obviously leaving him speechless with the way he held his mouth open in disbelief.

I knew I looked fierce but he looked just as good as I did. As a matter of fact, I wouldn't have minded if we just skipped dinner and stayed in all night for some good loving. But he and I cherished the moments we were able to get out on the town and have some real fun.

"So Calvin. Where are you taking me tonight?"

"Kesha. I'm taking you to this new jazz spot."

"The one downtown?"

"Yeah. I thought you'd like it."

"I do like the sound of that," I said joyfully as he escorted me by my hand.

Right after that, he and I sped to the restaurant. It had been a hard week. My job at the retail store was driving me crazy but it paid the bills. All I wanted to do was chill with Calvin and forget about the rest of the world. It managed to work by the time we sat down and started eating. I forgot about all my worries.

But no sooner did we sit down, did one of Calvin's friends come along and sit right beside us. It was his loud, obnoxious friend Craig who couldn't seem to keep himself out of jail for a minute. I personally paid no attention to Craig, but Calvin was a sucker for his friends. Whenever one of them asked him to jump, he'd ask them how high. That was my man's greatest weakness. He didn't know how to say no to his friends ever. Sometimes he'd miss dates with me and pass me over just to be with another one of his sorry ass friends.

I moaned under my breath as Craig instantly recognized him and the two began to discuss old times and some new things. I just sat there and drank my wine until I was tipsy before the food came. All Craig did was nod at me and I looked over at his trifling, chicken-headed girlfriend. Both those ghetto losers deserved each other. She didn't say anything to me and I went on eating while Calvin and Craig talked.

I was so annoyed and when Calvin noticed it, he quickly stopped his conversation and began focusing on me.

"I'm sorry baby. Craig is my boy. I haven't seen him in a couple of weeks so he and I had to catch up on things."

"I'm sure you had to," I sulked and rolled my eyes at him.

"Don't be like that Kesha. I'm sorry. I'm going to focus on us right now, Okay?"

The sound of his voice seemed sincere and so we got on with the rest of the night as if nothing had ever happened. He and I talked and we got as close as we had in the past. I forgave Calvin for ignoring me instantly. I never stayed mad at him for long.

For the rest of the night, he and I engaged in pleasant conversation. I knew that there was nothing that could take me away from Calvin. At least that was what I thought that night.

By the time we made it back to our apartment, I was ready for some serious loving. It didn't take long after before we were through the door, that I shed my clothes immediately. Calvin loved looking at how sexy my body appeared in lingerie. It was all he could do to keep his tongue in his mouth. I did a quick, sultry little strip tease to get his taste buds aroused. And it wasn't long before he was tasting me too. He wanted me more than he had wanted me before.

"Why don't you take everything off Kesha. I want to really see all of you. It's been on my mind all night."

I obliged his wishes and removed every last stitch of clothing on my body. Instantly, Calvin rose and took one of my nipples into his mouth. He sucked like a baby sucking for milk. I eased back in the couch and called out his name.

I was so wet inside I could barely wait. It seemed as if he couldn't either because before I knew it, he was ready to enter me and thrill me with his tender love muscle over and over again. I was ready for him as I stradled onto his lap and rode his manhood like a wild horse. He grabbed onto my hips, trying to steady the speed of them but it was useless. I had too much pent up passion to just hold it all inside. I wanted him more than I could express. The only signal of my affection came from my loud moans and sighs. Passion was burning up in every inch of my body.

"I'm coming," I screamed at the top of my lungs. I had reached the point of no return due to Calvin's skillful moves in the bedroom.

But I made sure my man wasn't disappointed. It wasn't before

61

long that he came to and we both melted together on the plush sofa. Sweat covered our bodies delicately. I nestled in his arms until the calm of the room lulled me to sleep. My fiance was incredibly good in bed. It wasn't the only thing he had going on for him, but it sure did matter when we got intimate with each other.

I spent the next day at work, chirping like a bird. All of my customers could tell that I was happy. It was like everyone knew that I had some ass the night before. My co-worker approached me during our lunch break. Regine had a wide grin on her face.

"I can tell somebody got some last night," she said.

I just looked at her and rolled my eyes playfully. "Of course. What can I say. I have a good man who knows how to keep his woman happy."

"Well that's good because there's enough of us out here who don't have a man that keeps them happy."

"You're turn is coming Regine. You know there's a fine man out there just waiting to meet you. You simply haven't come across him yet," I said confidently.

Regine finished with her lunch and stood up to get ready to go back on the floor. "Listen, I have work to do okay. And I'll take your word for it, but my man better hurry up and come soon. I'm losing patience."

I sat and stared into space after she left. I really was fortunate to have such a good man like Calvin. Most sisters could search their whole entire lives and not find anyone nearly as good as him. Right before I was going to get back to my shift, my cell phone rang. I answered it quickly, seeing that it was my man.

"Kesha."

"Hey Calvin, baby. What's up?" I asked.

"Well I know it's Friday and we planned on doing something together, but I have to take a reincheck on that."

"What do you mean?"

"I mean baby. I'm gonna go and hang out over Darryl's house tonight. Me, him and Craig are going to go out and celebrate one of our boy's birthdays."

I was sceptical and heated at the same time. The weekends were a big problem with Calvin and I. I never got a chance to see him when I wanted to. I worked so hard during the week and the weekends were usually the only time I had to really spend quality time with my man. I was sick of his damn friends getting in the way of our personal time.

"Well, whatever," I hollered. "If your friends are more important than me, then go ahead and do what you have to do. I'm not going to stop you."

Calvin sighed into the phone. "Kesha, please don't take this personally. I mean, I'm just going out with my friends."

"Are you sure all of y'all aren't going out for more than a good time, like to chill with some other females?" I could feel the steam coming from my ears as I asked the question.

He caught an instant attitude. "No Kesha. You know our relationship is too strong and I would never cheat on you. I don't know why you would even say such a thing."

Suddenly, I felt like I was tripping for no reason. I really needed to keep my cool. But it was hard. It seemed as if Calvin was choosing his friends over me every single weekend and I was beginning to feel neglected.

"Well fine Calvin. You go and do what you have to do. I'm going to go out with my girlfriends."

"Okay. See you should go out with your friends too," he urged.

"Sure honey. Whatever," I shouted before shutting my cell phone closed. I didn't want to hear another word he had to say to me. My heart was starting to close towards him.

I worked the rest of my shift and when the night was over, I immediately headed home. I didn't want to be with my girlfriends at all. All I wanted to do was sit on the couch and sulk like I usually did on the weekends. The apartment soon felt like a ghost town.

Soon I heard a knock at the front door. I got up to open it and to my surprise found and unknown man standing before me.

"I'm sorry to bother you, but are you Kesha?" the man asked.

"Yes," I replied.

"Sorry to disturb you. I'm Shawn. A friend of Calvin's. He wanted me to come by and pick up a jacket of his for tonight for the party I'm having."

"Oh so you're the friend who is celebrating his birthday."

"Yeah, I'm twenty-five today and I already feel like an old man. I'm not one for parties but I thought I'd throw one this year."

"Well, I better let you in. The closet is right there on the side, next to the kitchen." I didn't say another word as Shawn helped himself to the closet and retrieved the coat my man must've requested.

After that, he extended his hand, grabbing mine before kissing it gently. He seemed so sweet. He was like the gentleman myman used to be before his boys took priority over me. I wanted this man all of a sudden. I wanted to be with the man who made my body shiver in an instant. But it wasn't necessarily the impact he had on my body that made me want him. It was the fact that he was a true gentleman and didn't even seem interested in being at his own part. I sensed him as being even more mature than my boyfriend.

Well, I didn't say much else to Calvin when he came home but I did ask him a lot about Shawn. I found myself wanting my fiance's friend! And I couldn't help the amount of lust that was pouring out of my body. All of me wanted him like never before.

I played it off to Calvin and told him that I wanted to hook Shawn up with Regine from work. He bought it hook, line and sinker and I never had to explain another thing about the matter. He had given me more than enough information on Shawn. Before too long I knew where he lived and worked and what his personal interests were.

"But he doesn't hang out too much with the fellas," Calvin added. "I don't know if Regine would mind a man being up underneath her twenty-four seven."

"Oh she won't mind," I answered, knowing that I was talking about myself on the down low.

Pretty soon, it was like I was stalking him. I showed up at his job and sometimes camped outside his apartment. I saw him with a few women but none of them managed to make a lasting impression on him. But then I felt silly. What in the hell was I doing trying to get my fiance's man? I knew then that it was time to have a serious talk with him before our relationship went totally out the window. I knew Calvin and I had to have a serious talk.

As soon as I went home that night, I confronted my man. "Baby, I think you and I need to have a talk," I said.

Calvin pulled up a seat and examined the seriousness on my face. "What is it?"

"I'm thinking about leaving this relationship because I can't take how you choose your friends over me. This isn't going to work out if we keep up like this."

Calvin looked at me and nodded his head. "I admit I've been with my friends a lot here and there and I'm truly sorry for overlooking you and making you feel neglected. Is there anything I can do to make it up to you?"

"Yes," I exclaimed. "Just pay a little more attention to me that's all."

"I can try that. Because the last thing I want is to lose you. I want us to be together forever."

I simply agreed and our relationship began with a new start at that moment. It was like Calvin made a serious promise to keep his commitments to me. He was serious about all that he was putting his mind to and that made me very happy.

From that moment on, Calvin was like another man. I really didn't want to cheat on him and I knew that was the next step if he kept avoiding me. All I needed was his time and attention and I finally had it before it was too late.

THE END

INSATIABLE
I'm Addicted To Sex!

Two weeks after school ended in June, I packed up my car and headed for Martha's Vineyard on Cape Cod. Teaching fourth grade had never been stressful until this year and to make matters worse, New York was in the middle of a sweltering heat wave. I needed to get away from the city and my problems. A couple weeks on the ocean seemed like the perfect solution.

Once on the road, I began to relax. I left early on Sunday morning when the traffic was light. With every mile the tension in my shoulders eased and I wondered whether it was time to consider transferring to a new school. I loved teaching and I loved my school but the new principal had made my last year, the year from hell.

I pushed those thoughts from my mind and watched the traffic with more attention. Every time I thought about that man, my stomach tightened. According to him, we weren't working hard enough, and even worse, he wanted us to push the kids even more than ourselves. His attitude was so arrogant and abrasive, that many of the teachers had stopped attending staff meetings. Whenever anyone challenged him, he went out of his way to let everyone know that he had a Harvard degree and therefore knew more than you who had gone to teacher's college. By the middle of June, the kids weren't the only ones who couldn't wait for school to end.

A light rain began to fall forcing me to pay attention to the road. I turned off the tape player and put on the radio to distract me from my own thoughts. I was on vacation now. I took a couple of deep breaths and began to relax again.

It was too bad that I lost my temper during the last week of school. I probably shouldn't have stormed into his office like I did. Well, that was all over now. Maybe a new school was the answer. The rain was coming down harder as I began to think about my trip to Cape Cod.

Aunt Naomi's reunion was probably just what I needed to help me get over this last year. I planned to stay a week on Martha's Vineyard at one of the houses that Aunt Naomi had rented for everyone, and then spend another week traveling up and down the coast. Once I decided to attend this reunion, I went to the library and borrowed a couple of travel books on New England. I mapped out all the places I wanted to stop at and decided that I was going to go out on a boat too. I had never been on a boat, ever.

My Aunt Naomi was my mom's favorite sister. They were the two youngest in a family of eight. Of all the children, she was the only one who went to college and eventually married a doctor. She raised her five kids alone after he died. The last time I saw her was twelve years ago at my mother's funeral.

Well, according to her second husband Jaffer, some years back she got bitten by the family history bug. He said it was all Alex Haley's fault, because he got everyone interested in searching for ancestors after Roots was on television. Well, she got very excited when she traced some of our family back to before the Civil War. And then, after locating all these people in the past, she decided that there should be a family reunion of all this distant cousins and she was just the person to make it happen.

Her husband tried to talk her out of it, he told me on the phone a couple of months ago. He told her no one was going to come to a reunion of strangers, but she wouldn't listen. She wrote letters and phoned people until she contacted over a forty Waywards, Hudsons, Newmans and Jeffersons. My mother and my aunt were Jeffersons. No, she told me on the phone, we weren't related to Thomas Jefferson or his slave mistress, but she did find that both of my great grandfathers had fought in World War I. Anyway, once she got this idea about a reunion into her head, there was no stopping her.

While doing her research, Aunt Naomi learned that some of our ancestors had lived on Martha's Vineyard. Since she lived in Boston, she decided it would be the perfect place for the first ever family reunion. It took her months to make all the arrangements, which included renting one house with a dining room large enough for everyone to get together. At last count over twenty-four people had agreed to come.

On my drive north, I stopped in some of the small towns along the way. Many had at least one and sometimes two antique shops right on their main street. Now I don't have much extra money, but old dishes don't cost that much. The set my mother inherited from an aunt had lots of missing and chipped pieces in it. It would take me years to find all the pieces, but those dishes were the only thing that I had that belonged to my mother.

It was Tuesday afternoon, when I arrived at the Cape. The trip over to the island took almost an hour which I spent taking in the lovely sights and smelling the wonderful sea breezes. There wasn't much chance of getting lost, since Aunt Naomi had sent everyone a detailed map on where to go once we arrived on the island.

When I pulled into the driveway, a rather plumb woman with short white hair was there to meet us.

"Lora, dear, you are the image of your mother."

She placed her arms around me and gave me a warm hug. "She was about your age when I got married. I'll have to show you some family photos I have. Truly, you are image of your mother." I smiled and thanked her. I didn't own any photos of my mother as a young woman.

Whatever misgivings I had about meeting all these strangers now left me. I had hesitated before agreeing to come, because none of my brothers or sisters were coming. For me this really was a reunion with strangers much like Aunt Naomi's husband said. My mother's family was against her marrying my father, all except for my Aunt Naomi. My mother never spoke to any of her other brothers or sisters after she was married.

By the time I was born, all my siblings were already teenagers and by the time mama died, they had families of their own. When dad died two years later, I was on my own. I tried living with one of my older sisters for a few months, but it soon caused problems between her and her husband, so I moved out.

My Aunt Naomi now led me into a very large house. There was a wonderful smell coming from the kitchen.

"We decided to put you in one of the rooms on the very top floor. I hope you don't mind. Some of the older folks might not be able to make it up that last flight of stairs."

I smiled at her and said that was fine. "I'm so glad we going to get to know each other better. We need to make up for lost time starting right now," my Aunt said. And with that, she took me by the hand and led me into a large parlor.

"Everyone is going to get to take home one of these photo albums. It took me months of writing letters and lots of promising to return the originals—-before folks would let go of some of these."

There was a man sitting on one of the sofa's looking at a photo album. When we entered the room, he stood up to meet us. When I saw who it was, I froze to the floor. This had to be a dream, a bad dream. It was obvious that he was just as startled by my unexpected appearance.

"Lora, I want you to meet a very distant cousin of yours, Alan Arthur. I believe you share a great grandmother. "

"Alan, this is my niece, Lora Johnson."

"Aunt Naomi, I'm already acquainted with Mr. Arthur. He's the new principal of my school." All Alan Arthur said was "small world."

Just then the phone rang and Aunt Naomi excused herself to go answer it. I didn't know what to do so I just stood there. He spoke first.

"This collection of photos is incredible. Each one has a letter or paragraph with it, explaining who is in the picture and where and when it was taken." He was trying to ease the tension between us. It didn't work, so I turned to leave.

"Don't go, please. If we don't speak to each other all week, it's going to make it awkward for everyone else too. The last thing I want to do it ruin this reunion for the others."

He paused for a moment and then went on.

"Aunt Naomi has poured her heart and soul into this event, just think how hurt and disappointed she would be if we didn't all have a good time." When I didn't answer, he continued.

"Look, I know you don't like me but could we just declare a truce for this week. I will do my best to avoid you, but if we happen to be in the same room, couldn't we try and be civil to each other." I thought about his words.

"Your right, the last thing I want to do is hurt or disappoint Aunt Naomi. I accept your offer of truce and I too will be very civil to you for this next week."

He then stretched out his right hand toward me. "Deal?" I hesitated. I didn't want to shake his hand but I made a promise. I stepped forward and extended my hand. He held on to it longer than I thought necessary, but I didn't pull it away. When Aunt Naomi returned, he let it go.

"I think I'll take a walk before dinner, when do we eat?" Arthur directed his question to Aunt Naomi.

"We're waiting for two more families. They should be here within the hour. I'd say be back by 7:30."

"Seven-thirty it is." Alan then placed a small kiss on Aunt Naomi's cheek and left the room.

"For someone who had such a rough childhood, he's done so well for himself," my aunt said to me.

"Alan went to Harvard, Aunt Naomi, how hard could his childhood have been."

"You can't judge a book by it cover, Lora. The fact that he's turned his life around is nothing short of a miracle. The only reason he ended up at Harvard is because a teacher finally cared enough to get involved. It was clear that neither of his parents ever bothered. Why he was in and out of so many foster homes that by the time he was fourteen everyone had given up on him."

"So, who was this teacher that helped him?" I asked.

"He says it was a very strict hard driving social studies teacher he had when he got to high school. It seems he was also the boys' basketball coach. Wouldn't take any nonsense from any of the boys. He'd been in the Marines until a back injury forced him out early. Decided that what those kids needed more than love was discipline so they could learn to respect themselves. By the time he was a senior,

Alan had the grades and discipline to succeed at Harvard."

The phone rang again just then, and Aunt Naomi went to answer it. I decided I'd go into the kitchen and see if I could make myself useful.

My first dinner among these strangers was a lot of fun. Sixteen people squeezed themselves around a very long table and ate family style for what seemed like hours, telling stories in between mouthfuls. Along with the salad that I made, we had a huge pot of seafood chowder from the local fish market. Everyone took seconds of the sourdough bread, so they could get every bit of soup from their bowls as they listened to Aunt Naomi explained how she located all the people that were eating together that night. That wonderful smell that greeted me when I first entered the house, was our dessert, homemade peach cobbler.

When I finally settled into my bed that night, I wondered if real families ever had dinners like that.

Although Alan had been at the dinner table the night before, with so many people in between us, we never spoke. When I came down to breakfast the next morning, I learned that he had driven to the ferry landing to meet more of the incoming relatives. I helped bake pies all morning, something I never did at home.

When Alan came into the kitchen around lunch time, my aunt asked if he would drive to one of the markets on the other side of the island to pick up the lobsters she'd ordered for tonight's barbecue. Then, looking at me, she said, "Why don't you have Lora go with you to keep you company. She's been stuck here in the kitchen all morning, a nice drive along the ocean would be treat for her."

"I'd love to have Lora's company," he replied with a smile looking straight at me. His eyes said, ok now it's your move.

"I'll just take a minute to change," was all I said.

"I'll be out in the car, waiting."

I had been working in a T-shirt and shorts all morning and both were covered with cherry stains and flour. So was my face, when I looked in the mirror. I washed up and decided a long sleeveless dress would be more comfortable. As an afterthought, I put on open-toed sandals.

We didn't talk during the first fifteen minutes or so. We both pretended to be listening to the talk radio station that was on. Then Alan broke the ice.

"How about if we stop for lunch somewhere along here? When I came into the kitchen, I was really looking for something to eat." He was smiling at me, so I smiled back. "Sure, I'm hungry too."

We drove for another ten minutes when he spotted a very crowded parking lot off the side of the road. "That place looks pretty popular, want to give it a try?" I nodded and he pulled off the road.

The waitress seated us in a booth at the back of the restaurant then handed us menus and disappeared." I haven't had a fish taco in a long time." When the waitress reappeared, Alan ordered fish tacos for both of us. There was still some tension between us, so I tried to make some small talk.

"I really had a great time at dinner last night. I had no idea that I came from such a storytelling family. It wasn't like that when I was growing up." The words were out of my mouth before I knew it. Now I wished I could take them back. I didn't want Alan to know anything about me, nothing except that I was a good teacher.

When I didn't say anymore, Alan began. "I sat next to Cousin Rachel and her husband Paul. They told the funniest story about how they met in a San Francisco restaurant, each waiting for a blind date. By the time their dates finally arrived, it was too late. They had begun dinner without them."

When our food arrived, we exchanged stories about where we had last eaten fish tacos. Alan had a favorite place in Boston. Me, the last time I was in California, visiting a boyfriend stationed in San Diego. When we got back into the car, the tension between was gone. The rest of the drive was very pleasant and the lobsters were waiting for us when we arrived at the market.

A barbecue became iffy when late in the afternoon, rain clouds appeared. A vote of all family members was taking and all agreed that plans would not change unless there was a serious downpour. It never happened, so everyone ate and drank and told stories well past sunset.

After helping toast marshmallows for the little ones, I decided to take a stroll before heading back to the house. The earlier dusky sky was black except for the moon casting a beam on the water. Taking advantage of the romantic mood, several of the young couples were walking hand in hand. I was some distance from the family campfire, when Alan's voice stopped me.

"Can you give me a hand?"

I turned toward the direction of the voice. Clouds dimmed the moonlight, so all I could see was a silhouette. He was pulling a small sailboat out of the water while two of the children that had been with him took off running for the campfire. I walked toward him.

"Grab the end of the mast and help me carry it over there." His head motioned to a large deck high above the beach. I did as he asked. "Can you help me with the boat too?" I nodded and walked down into the surf. We carried the boat and placed it under the deck.

"Thanks, it would be have a lot harder to do it alone."

"No problem, I was glad to help."

"Mind if I walk with you?"

I hesitated for a second, then answered, "No of course not, but I'm getting cold and was heading back to the house."

In a single motion, he pulled off his sweatshirt and began pulling it over my head. "No, that's not necessary" was all I got out but by then the sweatshirt was covering my bare shoulders and arms. It was warm from his body heat and smelled of seawater. He rested his hands on my shoulders tentatively. I was glad it too dark for him to see my reaction. I had to admit to myself, this wasn't the first time I felt this way when standing close to him.

On the way back to the house, he told me that he had taken some of the youngsters out sailing earlier that afternoon and how these two had been napping and had missed out on the opportunity. So after dinner, he took them for a short sail so they wouldn't feel left out. This was a side of Alan Arthur I couldn't have imagined a week ago.

"My room's on the top floor," I said as we entered through the front door.

"So is mine."

I then headed up the stairway a couple of steps ahead of him. When I reached my room, I made a motion to take off his sweatshirt.

"I won't be needing it tonight," he said placing his hands on my shoulders to keep me from pulling it off. His eyes gazed down at me for a few seconds before his lips brushed against mine. "I've wanted to do that for months, Ms. Johnson," he said then kissed me harder. After a few seconds I came to my senses and pulled back. Alan then took his hands off my shoulders with an exaggerated motion, bowed his head slightly and said, "good night."

I couldn't sleep, thinking about how I had reacted to him. I had actually responded to his kiss. I tossed and turned for sometime and finally decided to go down to the kitchen for a cup of herbal tea. I didn't feel like dressing so I pulled Alan's sweatshirt over my nightgown and head down the stairs, barefoot.

Gingerly balancing my teacup on a saucer, I headed back up the stairs but even in the darkened hallway, I could see he was standing outside his room. I detected the smoky scent of Scotch as I moved past him.

"I've changed my mind. I want my sweatshirt back."

"I thought you said you didn't need it tonight."

"I afraid I might forget it in the morning."

"I'll have to put down my teacup."

He then stepped towards me and took the saucer and teacup and placed them atop the glass he was holding. I pulled off the sweatshirt and immediately felt a shiver of cold. My thin cotton nightgown provided no protection and my bare feet were becoming numb. I held out the sweatshirt but he didn't take it. Instead he moved closer. When

71

the Scotch hit my nostrils and I moved back.

"It seems that I don't have a spare hand," he said motioning to his hands holding the teacup, saucer and glass of Scotch. "Would you mind putting in my room?" The door was open so I walked in and placed the sweatshirt on the bed.

"It's my favorite sweatshirt. It was a graduation gift from friend." Then looking at me for a few moments, he added in a softer voice, "I'm sorry, I violated our truce. I'll leave first thing in the morning so you don't have to keep trying to be civil to me."

"Wait, you can't leave. You've only been here three days. Aunt Naomi will never forgive me if she finds out you left because of me."

Standing there in the cold, I was overwhelmed with feelings of fear. I didn't want to loose the family I had just found. The thought of my aunt being angry with me suddenly overwhelmed me with sorrow and dread.

"Look, please don't leave. I will do anything you ask, if you stay." I had to make him change his mind, so I took a step toward him. "I'll even transfer to another school in the fall, so it's I who will be out of your life permanently. Just don't go, please."

"You won't need to do that, I've already resigned. I'm going back to Boston."

"You've taken another job? But you've only been with us one year, how's that going to look on your resume?"

"Now why would that matter to you, Ms. Johnson. The last time you stormed into my office, you made it quite clear that as head of the Teachers Union, you were going to the Board of Trustees to file a grievance against me."

"I sorry about that. Truly I am. I acted impulsively and found out later that the information I was given was incorrect. I came to your office to apologize the next day, but you'd already left for the summer."

"I'd left never to return, Ms. Johnson. Much as it bothered me, I finally accepted the idea that you and I couldn't work together much less become friends."

I had taken back my teacup which now chattered against the saucer. I couldn't feel my feet. My whole body began to shiver. Alan, putting down his glass of Scotch moved toward me, taking the teacup from my hands once again.

"You're freezing. You have to get into bed." His arms pushed me out of his room and into mine where he covered me with a blanket as soon as I slipped into bed. He then left the room momentarily and returned carrying his sweatshirt. "Put it on," he commanded. He then began to rub my feet with his hands. He rubbed them until I stopped shivering.

"I'm going to go downstairs and get you something hot to drink." Within a few minutes, he was back with a mug of cider flavored with something stronger.

"What's in this?"

"Never mind, just drink it."

It burned slightly on it's way down. I took several more swallows and I felt tears welling up in my eyes. Alan had gone back to rubbing my feet and was startled when he looked up.

"Don't cry, please don't cry," he said as his thumbs wiped the tears from my cheeks. "I'll stay a few more days and no one will blame you when I leave."

I placed my hand over his and told him how really sorry I was for treating him so badly this past year. Then I moved forward and place a kiss on his lips. He hesitated a moment and pulled back to gaze into my eyes.

"I didn't put that much brandy in the cider."

"It's not the brandy." I leaned forward again and this time he returned my kiss. As the heat of the brandy mixed with the heat in his lips, and my head began to swim.

"I thought that only happened in the movies."

"What?

"A man's kiss making you dizzy."

"Am I making you dizzy?

"Yes, very."

"Good, because you've been making me crazy for months." He then kissed me long and hard. "And given me sleepless nights, too."

Moments later, Alan got up and turn off the lights. For a moment I thought he was going to leave the room and I realized that wasn't what I wanted him to do. When he slid in beside me, the dizziness quickly returned. Pulling off the sweatshirt, he told me he would see to it that I wouldn't be needing it anymore tonight.

I was surprised at how quickly I was responding to his touch. A body that only moments before was shivering with cold, now was pulsing with heat. Delicious feelings covered my entire body after he gingerly slid my nightgown off my shoulders and down over my hips. His fingers skimmed over my neck and shoulders electrifying me down to my once numb toes. His lips moved slowly from the hallow of my neck to the space between my breasts.

"Every time you would storm into my office, I wanted to come out from behind my desk, close the door and moved you up against the wall. I wanted to take those hands of yours that were always flying in the air and hold them above your head so you couldn't fight me any more and then I wanted to take my mouth and cover yours so you'd stop shouting at me. Then I wanted all that heat and passion to simmer down to a low boil and have it come out in a totally different way."

"As a principal you're not allowed to do that to a teacher."

"Ms. Johnson, if you knew what I did to you in my fantasies you'd be blushing in the dark."

He kissed me again and then with a gentle motion pushed me onto my stomach. Straddling me, he stroked and kissed my neck, my shoulders, and then my back. His hands moved lower, over my curved hips, lower still. "Mind if I turn up the heat?" he whispered in to my ear. I answered by rolling back to face him. "How hot can you make it?" I asked uncurling myself like a languid cat.

He was a gentle and considerate lover, paying close attention to the sounds I made. Occasionally he'd warn me about what he was going to do next. When the small of my back arched instinctively, he asked if I was ready to have that fire put out. "Yes," I answered. He was as open and free in his own pleasure as I was in mine. Afterward, he gave me the most gentle of kisses.

Raising himself on one elbow, he smiled at me. "The real you is so much better than any fantasy I created." He then pulled me closer to him, folding me into his arms tightly.

When our bodies cooled, he retrieved the blanket and sheet that I had thrown to the floor. Not much later, we both feel into a deep sleep.

I awoke to Alan stroking my hair. He had already showered. His hair was damp, and I could smell toothpaste when he kissed me.

"Rise and shine, honey. We're going sailing."

"Sailing?"

"Yup. Aunt Naomi told me you've never been on a boat. Well, that's going to change today. Now hurry up and get dressed. Oh, wear a bathing suit under your shorts. Your pretty bottom is going to get wet. And bring a hat."

The small sailboat was already on the beach, its sail flapping in the early morning breeze. Alan showed me where to sit and how to fold my legs. With a massive push of his body, the little craft slipped off the sand and into the water. Alan then jumped in and pulled in the sail. Suddenly, we were skimming over the water. With the sun warming my face, I was filled with an overwhelming sense of joy and serenity.

Watching Alan maneuvering the rudder and sail so easily, I asked, "When did you learn to sail?"

"In college. I had a good friend whose family owned a large sailboat. I found that being out on the water was very relaxing."

"I think I could get used to this," I smiled at him as I waved my arms in the sunlight and sea breeze."

"Good, because I could certainly use a mate on my boat. You know, to swab the decks, fetch the water, cook the food."

"Do you own a boat?"

74

"No, not yet, but I plan to one day. Mostly, I just rent one for weekends in the summertime. You'll have to move to Boston, if you want the mate job."

"What about my job?"

"Boston has plenty of jobs for caring, hardworking teachers. I even know a guy who can give you a good recommendation."

We sailed for most of the morning with Alan detailing the sites and landmarks for me. Locating an isolated spot along the shore, he beached the boat. To my surprise, he took a thermos and beach towel from under a tarp, then headed me toward an abandoned boat ramp.

"You've been here before."

He answered my question with a smile and helped me climb down under the structure. Through the broken slats, you could see up and down the entire beach.

"It's the kind of hiding place a young boy might take advantage of when he didn't want to be found." Alan volunteered. "I spent one summer here with a very nice foster family. If I'd been smarter, I could have grown up here, learning to sail many years earlier." He then leaned over and kissed me.

We spread out the beach towel and Alan unscrewed the thermos. "Ice tea?" he offered. "You are the perfect tour guide," I replied as I leaned over and kiss him. After a long kiss, he pulled back, face serious.

"Why were you so angry with me all last year?"

"You don't know?"

"No, I truly don't know."

"It was your attitude towards the students, your arrogance and if you must know, your philosophy of teaching." I tried to say it as nicely as I could, but clearly my words stung. "Go on," was all he said.

"I didn't agree with you that we weren't working hard enough and that the kids needed to be pushed harder. As head of the teachers' union, I know how hard those teachers work and how little respect they get from the parents and public. I just wasn't going to let some Harvard educated type come in and tell us that we were all lazy and unproductive."

"I never said that about you or any of the other teachers."

"You may not have said it out loud, but that's how you came across in staff meetings."

"Lora, one of the things I did learn at Harvard, was that men and woman communicate differently. What I said and what you heard were not the same thing. But I didn't know that my communication style was that far off the mark." He hesitated for a moment and then added, "I want to succeed at this new school. I would appreciate your help in keeping me from repeating my mistakes."

"That'll be hard, with me in New York and you in Boston."

Reaching over, Alan took both of my hands into his. He then kissed my fingertips. "I was very serious about being my mate. I'm in love with you, have been for months. Last night took care of any doubts I might have had."

I sat in stunned silence. "But we barely know each other."

"Lora, we known all the important things. We know that we both care about teaching, about children, about family. We know the kind of family we come from and the kind of family we want to have."

I didn't know how to answer him. Only three days ago, I couldn't think of anything kind to say about this man. Now, I was thinking of marrying him. This was crazy.

"Yesterday you learned that I can keep you warm on very cold nights and I learned, that the real Lora is so much better than any fantasy. Today you learned that you love to sail, and I just happen to be planning to buy a sailboat." He stopped long enough to smile at me. There was such tenderness in his eyes.

"For years I've been looking for a woman that shared my priorities and my values. The more I worked with you, the more I knew you were that woman. A few days ago, I thought I'd lost you forever. I don't want to risk that again." He kissed me softly, stroking my face.

All I could do is shake my head in confusion. "This is so sudden. I'm not sure I'm ready to make such a decision."

"I understand that. You can take all the time you want to make your decision. I won't rush you, I promise."

Taking a more direct route, we sailed back in silence. When we reached the house, Aunt Naomi greeted us with a warm hug. "We're all having lunch in the dining room —in about an hour. Hope you can join us." It would take me that much time to clean up.

Grateful for my private shower, I stood under steaming hot water to wash off sand, sweat and ice tea. I was surprised when the bathroom door open and Alan stepped in. Taking of his robe, he was clearly ready to join me.

"I thought I'd come and help you work up a lather. I know how to do it. I've been practicing in those fantasies I told you about."

How could I not love this man? His sense of humor alone was priceless. Opening the shower door, I motioned for him to enter. Handing him the soap, I leaned back against the shower wall. "Well, let's see how much you know."

As he had hinted, he was a man with experience. He told me to close my eyes, turn to the wall, and take a deep relaxing breath. I could feel his large soapy hands skimmed over my neck, my shoulders. He rubbed them with the experience of a professional masseuse. Then

76

"I'm sorry you had to see that, Dr. Davis." I said.

"I told you that you could call me Tony." He pulled up a chair to my desk and sat down. "Now tell me what is wrong."

"One of the nurses is giving me a hard time because the nursing home won't accept a patient until tomorrow," I explained. "So he has to stay here an extra day."

"Who was the nurse?" He asked.

"It's not important. I don't want you fighting my battles for me Dr. Davis, I mean Tony.""

"I just want to let the nurses know that everything that can be done is being done," he offered.

"Tony, thanks, but no thanks. Leave it alone." I didn't want him trying to run to my aid. I had a professional reputation to uphold.

"I hate to see you so stressed. After work why don't you have dinner with me and then afterward I can give you a massage."

I was stunned for a moment. As much as I would love to have that man's hands all over my body, I didn't want to compromise my position there by having an inappropriate relationship with one of the doctors. I didn't know where he was going with this, but I went back to my professional demeanor.

"I appreciate the offer, but I don't think that would be a good idea," I said, even though my body said otherwise.

"I'm not trying to come on to you," he said emphatically. "I am a certified massage therapist as well as a doctor. The massage would be therapeutic. The dinner invitation was just to break the ice prior to the massage." He stood up and walked to the front of my desk. "If you'd like, I could bring some Chinese food to your place and you can make up your mind about the massage while we eat. Besides, I have a lot of questions I want to ask about the hospital anyway."

The offer seemed innocent enough, so I accepted with hesitation. He reiterated that he wasn't going to try anything. A small part of me was hoping he would try something afterall.

And with that I gave him my address. He said he would be there around seven o'clock and left to go back to work.

The rest of my day was just as bad as earlier. By the time I left, I was so mad I could spit nails.

I'd been a social worker at the hospital for six years and I had never had a worse day. My supervisor had been all over me. We had a lot of discharges that day and I had to set up transportation to get the patients back to the nursing home. I had also been assigned five new patients. One of them was a pregnant teenager on crack, who was being a spoiled brat. For some reason everyone was getting on my nerves, from the doctors and nurses to the patients.

But to make matters worse, I didn't want to go home. I hated long, slow strokes covered my back and hips. After a little while, I felt both his hands encircling each leg. Slowly his hands moved up and down over and over again. Then there was a soft whisper, "turn around." By the time he touched my breasts, I was enveloped in the most delicious sensation of warmth and desire. "I think we'd better rinse me now," I said keeping my eyes closed.

Seconds later we toweled each other dry, all the while moving toward the bed. The sweet smell of floral soap lingered on his skin. "My turn," I whispered, as my hands now covered his body the way his had only moments before covered mine. I tried to take my time, but the heat between us rose quickly. It was different from the night before, more impatient, more intense, more demanding by both. Moments later we lying in each other's arms.

We were only a few minutes late for lunch. Most everyone was seated but not everyone had been served. During the meal, there was a lull in the conversation, so I announced that I had decided to move to Boston. I was smiled at Alan went I said it. Everyone cheering and congratulated us. Aunt Naomi was beaming, obviously delighted with her matchmaking skills. Smiling at both of us, she said,

" That is wonderful news. I'm so happy you'll be close by, so you can help me plan next year's reunion."

When I looked at Alan, he was smiling. He then took my hand and raised it to his lips. Look back at Aunt Naomi he said. "You can count on both of us to help make it happen."

THE END

HOUSE CALLS

I looked at the paperwork to move Mr. Johnson and shook my head in disgust. I had just gotten the call from the nurse on Unit 3. She was yelling at me about Mr. Johnson being discharged and that another patient was being brought to room 308. I had explained to her that the move couldn't take place because the nursing home he was being transferred to wouldn't be ready for him until the next day. Because she was so persistent, I tried one last time to make the patient transfer happen, but was unsuccessful. Knowing I had to call her back and let her know he couldn't be moved, I took a deep breath and made the call.

A friendly nurse answered the phone.

"Could I speak to the charge nurse please?" I hoped she was gone for the day, but no such luck.

"This is Mrs. Smith." Even her voice tore through me.

"Mrs. Smith, this is Denise in Social Services. In regards to Mr. Johnson, the nursing home is not prepared to accept him until tomorrow."

"This is totally unacceptable." She said, yelling in my ear. "There is no reason for that man to lay up in her another day. It is a waste of my time and my nurse's time. You are not doing your job."

I was pissed at the way she was speaking to me and found myself yelling back at her.

"Wait a minute now, I am doing my job. If they can't take him, what do you want me to do about it? Why don't you call them and make them take him?" I said defiantly.

"That is not my job," she commented, mumbling something about me being incompetent and immediately hanging up the phone in my ear.

I was so angry that I slammed the phone down, hurting my hand. As I was doing that, Dr. Davis walked in.

"Hey, hey, hey, what is going on? Why are you so upset?" he asked. He had obviously witnessed me throwing the phone around out of disgust.

Dr. Davis was this fine, dark brother that worked in the emergency department. He was about 6'1", muscular, with curly hair, and dimples. He made my panties wet every time I saw him.

He had been working at the hospital for about 6 months. We first met when he referred an elderly lady to social services for possible elder abuse. I made sure I had many consultations with him on other patients after that.

going home to an empty apartment. I had been separated from my boyfriend of five years for about a month, basically, because he was married. I couldn't stand him going home to her any longer. But I couldn't seem to get him off of my mind.

When I got home, I ran a hot bath, and soaked, trying to relieve my stress. After my relaxation efforts were over, I put on some panties and a tee shirt and stretched out on my sofa and watched the news.

I was extremely tired, especially since I hadn't slept well the night before. Around two in the morning, I woke up horny as hell. My nipples were so hard, they could have cut glass.

No male attention had come my way in a while and I was desperately in need. I made the mistake of calling my ex's cell phone, hoping that he would be in the mood for one last steamy sex session for the road. I really missed how his big, rough hands felt on my breasts and how good it felt when he buried his face between my legs. Good lawd, he knew exactly how to please me. The feeling he gave me when he plunged his manhood deep inside my love, always caused me to scream in ecstasy.

While reminiscing about our last night together, I replayed the events in my head. Jimmy had come over to my apartment wanting to talk about how much he loved me and what a mistake it was to marry Kathy. We sat out in his SUV to give us a little privacy since my roommate was home.

Money problems was the main complaint that kept coming up in their marriage. Kathy was spending more money than what was coming in and Jimmy was more than frustrated by it. If she had a good job, making good money like me, he would be a very happy man.

We moved closer together and began kissing and his hand moved under my dress and caressed my bare legs. Feeling his arousal with my hand made me get wet. After unzipping his pants and setting him free, I pleasured him with my mouth, and the feeling it gave me was incredible. He loved it too.

The oral loving continued as his hands continued up behind me, only to find that I didn't have panties on. We moved the party to the back seat so that I could straddle him and let him slowly guide his manhood into me. It was good, slow grind, but the feeling was too good and the pace quickened. The top of my dress was unbuttoned and my breasts fell free. He sucked my nipple into his mouth as my body continued to move up and down his shaft. It didn't take long before we both exploded. Remembering that caused me to have a major throbbing between my legs and I needed somebody to put the fire out.

I called Jimmy's number, but there was no answer. He was probably asleep, cuddled up with that bitch he married.

Frustration caused me to sneak into my roommates room while

she was sleeping, take her vibrator out of her night stand drawer, and go back into my room and pleasure myself until I fell asleep, somewhat satisfied. It was good, but it didn't take the place of a man's touch.

I dosed off for a while, but was awakened by the doorbell ringing. After looking through the peephole and seeing Tony, I realized that I had completely forgotten about him coming over. After running into the bedroom and putting on some shorts, I ran back and opened the door. Tony was standing there looking incredibly handsome, wearing a maroon polo shirt and black slacks. He was holding a bag of Chinese food.

"Hi," I said, attempting to fix my clothes and hoping I looked presentable. "I completely forgot about you coming over. Please come in."

"Thanks." he said as he walked past me. "I brought dinner." He held the bags up in the air.

"Great, I'm starved." I grabbed a couple of plates from the kitchen and started to unpack the food. This was the first opportunity I'd had to see Tony in regular everyday clothes. Since I was used to seeing him wearing scrubs or a lab coat, it was nice to see him in casual attire.

Tony and I enjoyed pleasant conversation. He asked a lot of questions about the hospital and the relationship between Social Services and the doctors and nurses. I explained to him exactly what my duties as a Social Worker were. He seemed intrigued that I was so knowledgeable about my job.

I also learned a lot about Tony. He told me that his mother had died of a heart attack when he was a teenager, which prompted him to become a doctor. He wanted to do whatever he could to keep anyone else from losing his or her mother prematurely.

I had noticed him staring at my chest, so I looked down and realized that I had forgotten to put on a bra. My nipples were standing at attention. Although I was somewhat embarrassed, I was flattered at the visual attention he was giving my chest.

After the meal, we cleaned up our mess and sat back down in the living room.

"So, are you ready for the massage?" he asked.

I knew that question was coming eventually. After about thirty minutes of convincing, I finally relented. I got some towels and spread them out on the floor. Tony heated a bottle of baby oil in the microwave.

"I need you to undress and wrap this towel around you."

The thought of taking my clothes made me a little nervous, but I undressed in the bedroom and returned wearing the towel.

He gave me his word that he would not try to take advantage of me, or break the boundaries of our friendship. I laid down on my stomach on the towels and tried to relax. Tony moved the towel down off of my back and up from legs, just leaving my butt covered. The massage started at my feet as he gently massaged my feet and ankles, and slowly moved up to my calves.

His hands felt so good as he gently moved upward to my thighs, slightly opening my legs to massage the inner thigh on each leg. I started throbbing again and a slow moan escaped my lips.

"Are you okay?"

"Wonderful," I whispered.

My breathing became erratic when the massage reached the top of my thighs, so he stopped. He moved up to my shoulders and neck, gently massaging and slowly moving down to my upper back and then my lower back, all the way to the small of my back.

"That feels incredible," I told him.

"Do you want me to do the front?" He asked as he continued to massage my back.

"Mmmm, yes." My body was on fire, and I couldn't say no to anything he asked.

He rolled me over and removed the towel. I could tell he was mesmerized by my breasts. My eyes were closed as he applied the baby oil and began to massage my chest and breasts. My body started moving uncontrollably. He moved down to my belly and below. He continued to rub my body until I was completely covered in oil.

As he moved back up, he paid particular attention to my breasts until my body began to move very seductively. My nipples were incredibly hard and I was in my own world. He moved back down to my legs and massaged them again, but when he got to the top of my legs, I parted them and his hand slipped between my thighs and to my most intimate body part. I closed my legs around his hand. He began to massage me their slowly with one hand while massaging my breasts with the other. Twenty minutes later, my body stiffened, I moaned, then relaxed releasing his hand.

I just laid there quietly while my breathing returned to normal. He went into the bathroom and ran a hot bubble bath.

He helped me into the bathroom and into the tub. I laid my head back and fell asleep. When I woke up, I was still in the tub and Tony had gone home.

He was probably upset about me having an orgasm from his therapeutic massage. I felt so embarrassed.

I didn't know how I was going to be able to face him at work. I didn't mean for it to happen, but it felt so good, I couldn't help it.

The next day, I called in sick. I was just too embarrassed to go to work, even though I knew I would have to face him eventually. I just didn't want it to be then. The good part about it was I managed to clean my apartment from top to bottom. It was all I could think to do to keep from concentrating on the humiliation I was feeling about what had happened with Tony.

Later that afternoon, Tony rang my doorbell. He probably wanted to tell me how upset he was about my behavior the night before. After several moments, I finally opened the door.

"Tony, what are you doing here?"

"I came to apologize," he said.

I was confused. I thought I was the one that needed to apologize.

"Come in. Have a seat." I waved him inside and he brushed by me. His touch sent a chill up my spine. "I don't know what you are apologizing for but..."

"I'm sorry for my behavior last night," he interrupted. "You put your trust in me to be professional and I betrayed that trust. I hope you can forgive me. If you file a complaint with Administration, I'll understand."

I didn't know what he was talking about. File a complaint about what? Why would I file a complaint on a man that made me have one of the best orgasms I've ever had?

"I assure you that no complaint will be coming from me," I said sincerely. "I didn't feel you did anything wrong. My behavior, on the other hand, left a lot to be desired. I hope I didn't offend you."

"Of course not," he responded and I was relieved.

I watched his eyes trail my body, stopping to examined my breasts standing at attention beneath the T-shirt I wore. I definitely had to start wearing a bra at home, especially if he kept paying me visits.

"So Doc, did you need to talk to me about anything else?" I asked.

He smiled. "Well, now that you mention it, I would like to invite you to lunch. Are you hungry?"

"Actually, I'm starving. Let me change and I'll be right with you." With that I ran into my bedroom and searched in my closet for something cute to wear, choosing a simple orange and white, flowery sundress, once again omitting the bra, since he was very interested in my breasts. I accented my outfit with sandals, showcasing my toes were freshly painted. I ran my fingers through my hair and was ready to go.

We went to a nice Italian restaurant. It was quite beautiful inside. The air conditioner was kicking, causing my nipples to stand up, but I didn't mind because it gave the good doctor something to look at. After we ate, we took a walk in the park to help our food digest. He asked me if I had a boyfriend and I told him all about my relationship with Jimmy. I asked him if he had someone special in his life.

"No. I was engaged a couple of years ago, but she died." He spoke in a lower tone than I had gotten used to him sounding. I didn't know what to say. He walked over to a bench and sat down, with me following closely behind.

"We were out riding on my motorcycle with the motorcycle club I belonged to. There were about fifteen bikes in the group. Out of nowhere, two guys on Ninja bikes flew past our group. The had to be going at least one hundred miles per hour. Anyway, they cut in front of our lead bike. They were looking back at us laughing. One of them drifted over and hit the other one causing him to lose control and fall, which caused a chain reaction. Bikes started going all over the road. The bike in front of us fell. We hit that bike and fell. My girlfriend got up and tried to run to the side of the interstate, but she didn't make it." Tears began to stream down his face and I wanted to reach out and kiss his tears away.

"She was hit by a car and killed instantly," he explained.

I was blown away. "I'm so sorry," was all I could say.

"So anyway, I haven't dated since then," he continued. "I haven been able to ride again either. But I have had the urge to ride lately."

"I've never been on a motorcycle."

"Would you like to?" he asked.

"Sure."

"How about Saturday? We can take a ride out into the country."

"Sounds great."

He took me back to my apartment and walked me to the door. I thanked him for lunch. He gave me a light kiss on the lips and thanked me for listening. I was surprised and excited by the kiss.

Since I hadn't seen him the rest of the week, I wondered if we were still on for the motorcycle ride. I got up on Saturday and got dressed so I could be ready at the time Tony had originally specified. Within moments, he was ringing my doorbell.

"I was wondering if you were going to cancel on me," I said playfully.

"Not on your life," he said, flashing me a sexy grin. "Ready to go?"

"Yep. Just let me grab my jacket."

Tony looked good in black jeans and a black tee shirt he was wearing. The muscles in his arms and chest shone perfectly through the thin shirt. He was so sexy. I couldn't wait to get on the back of his motorcycle and wrap my arms around his body.

We traveled about three hours, but it seemed like only a few minutes. I was loving the feeling of so much power between my legs. The vibration was making me horny. Not to mention my arms around that fine man. I pressed my breasts against his back hoping he would notice how much I was enjoying being with him. He took us through a wooded area and then to a beautiful lake. We stopped there. He opened up one saddlebag and pulled out a thick blanket and spread it out on the ground.

Then he pulled out lots of food from the other saddlebag. I couldn't believe he cooked all of this food. We had fried chicken, containers of baked beans, potato salad and mashed potatoes and gravy. He even had cold sodas.

"So what do you think?" he asked.

"I can't believe you did all of this."

"Well, riding gives me a big appetite. And I cooked it all myself."

"I'm impressed. And I'm hungry."

We ate as much as we could, then went for a walk around the lake. It was so peaceful. Not another person in sight.

We walked close to the water. Tony was trying to show me a fish in the water, or so I thought. I leaned over to get a better look when Tony pushed me. But he grabbed me just before I hit the water. I grabbed a hand full of water and threw it in his face and ran back towards the blanket. He caught me just as I reached the blanket and tackled me. He fell on me and started tickling me. I thrashed around begging him to stop.

Then out of nowhere, he kissed me. I was completely taken by the softness of his kiss. He started slow, little light kisses, then he slid his tongue into my mouth, nice and smooth, not rushed at all. I was lost in his kiss.

I could feel the heat coming from his body. Our passion grew. He rolled me over on top of him and lifted my sweater and fondled my breasts through my bra. I took the sweater off. He kissed me again and took my bra off. I leaned over his face so that he could take my nipples into his mouth, one and then the other. He sucked my nipples like a hungry puppy.

The sensation drove me wild. I pulled his tee shirt off and returned the favor. I could feel his hardness through his jeans as I left a trail of kisses from his chest to his belly button.

I loosened his jeans and he maneuvered out of them. I took him into my mouth. He gasped from the feeling. I took my time, long slow strokes. He let out a moan of pleasure. I stroked him with my hand as I sucked him in. His moans became louder.

His hips rose off of the blanket. I felt his hands pulling on the back of my head.

"Oh my God!" he screamed as he exploded.

I rested my hand on his chest as he regained his composure. I could feel his heart racing as I laid my head on his chest.

"Girl, you tried to kill me," he joked.

85

"No baby, I don't want you to die. I just want to please you." I kissed him. He rolled me on my back and laid his sexy body on mine. He gave me a long sensual kiss.

"You know, I could get used to this."

"I hope you do. I'm not going anywhere unless you ask me to."

He started kissing me again, giving me soft kisses on my face and ears. He nibbled on my earlobes. He left a wet trail of kisses on my neck and chest. He sucked my nipples into his mouth. He took his time loving my breasts. It felt incredible.

I was drowning in the wetness my body had accumulated from being aroused. Tony kissed my thighs and then licked the center of me. He felt so good. He stroked my nipples with his thumbs as he loved me with his mouth. It didn't take long for me to lose control. I raked my nails across his back and squeezed his head between my thighs as I climaxed time and time again. I thought it would never stop. I had never had a multiple orgasm before. Just as I thought the end was near, he stopped licking me and moved his body on top of mine and slid his manhood deep inside of me.

"Oh baby, oh God, oh my!!!" I screamed as he moved in and out of me.

"Am I hurting you?" he asked.

"No, please don't st st stop."

His pace began to quicken. I matched him stroke for stroke. Sweat was pouring from both of our bodies. I know he made me sweat my perm out. I licked his ears and kissed his neck.

I put my hands on his butt and tried to pull him deeper inside of me. He felt so god. He pulled out a little and started moving in fast, short strokes, then long deep strokes. He pulled completely out, and turned me over on my knees. He entered me from behind, pulling on my hips with every stroke.

I reached between my legs and felt his rod going into me. I squeezed his testicles gently as he moved in and out of me.

He reached around me and squeezed one of my breasts. His pace picked up.

His strokes became erratic. I couldn't hold back any longer. I arched my back and screamed as my orgasm hit hard. My screams and moans sent him over the edge. He pulled me hard against as he released all of his love juices into me. His body jerked as he lost control.

We laid naked in each other's arms for several minutes.

"You are incredible." he said and kissed the tip of my nose.

"Is that a good thing, Doc?"

"It is a great thing."

"So, will I get to see you anymore after today?" I was fishing for a commitment.

"Denise, I don't want to spend another day not seeing you."

Tony and I began to see each other exclusively. A part of me was wondering if I had fallen too quickly for him but I fought with myself to enjoy all the attention Tony was giving me. At work, we maintained a professional appearance and no one knew about our relationship. Away from the job, he took me to restaurants I'd never been to before and took me to plays and concerts. He introduced me to a new culture, while taking the time to do things that I liked. We had a great time.

Everything was going well with us until I got a phone call one evening.

"Hi, Baby, long time no hear from." I recognized Jimmy's voice instantly.

"What do you want?" I said coolly.

"Why so hostile? I know it's been a while since I've called, Baby, but I can explain."

"No need to explain."

"I want to. You need to hear this. Don't you still love me?" he asked.

"Jimmy, I haven't heard from you in weeks, and now you are bugging me about love. Where have you been and why haven't you answered my calls?"

"Baby, I'm on my way over, I'll explain everything when I get there."

He hung up and was at my door thirty minutes later. I really didn't want to see Jimmy. I was falling in love with Tony and for the first time in years I was happy.

"You look great," he said giving me the once over, admiring the silk pajama set I was wearing. I wasn't expecting company. Besides, Jimmy has seen all of me many times.

"I really don't have time for this. Say what you have to say." I wanted to get rid of him. I never could be around him long without something sexual happening.

"Look, I've been having a lot of personal problems lately. Kathy and I have been going at like cats and dogs, and I've been slammed at work." He explained. "Kathy came home last night and really gave me hell and said she was leaving. I haven't seen her since, and don't want to. You are the woman I love and the woman I want to be with. Just say the word, Niecy, and I'm yours."

I loved to see a man beg. But his timing couldn't have been worse.

"Jimmy, I know you love me, and a part of me will always love you, but we can't be together. Our timing is off. Now you are free, but I'm not. I have someone in my life now." I said hoping he would accept that and leave.

"Oh really? Who is it?" he asked. He was hurt, but not giving up.

"It doesn't matter. You don't know him. He treats me right and most importantly, he was here for me. You weren't."

"I'm here now. Niecy, I love you and you love me. We belong together." I was sucker for Jimmy whenever he was begging but not this time.

"I used to think that nobody would be able to make me feel as good as you use to, but I was wrong." I said, trying to piss him off so he would leave. But my plan backfired.

He slapped me with such force, I fell backward across the coffee table. He snatched me up and started trying to kiss me and fondle my breasts. I fought to get away, but he was too strong.

He threw me down on the couch and laid on top of me. He tried to kiss me again. He put his hand in my top and squeezed my breast.

"Does he do this to you?" he asked with venom in his voice.

I didn't know what to do. I looked around for something to hit him with, but couldn't reach anything. He raised up a little so that he could put his hand in my pants. That was the opportunity I needed. I raised my knee up as hard as I could and kicked him in the groin. He screamed in pain and rolled onto the floor. I got up, got my keys and ran out the door to my car. Just as I got in and locked the door, he was there.

"Open the door!" He yelled. "I'm not going to hurt you."

I started the engine.

"Don't do this. Open the door. I'm sorry."

"You're crazy." I screamed.

"Open the damn door, now!" he ordered.

"No!!"

He raised his foot up and kicked the glass in. Glass shattered all over me. I floored it before he could reach inside. I didn't know where I was going, but I had to get away from him. It didn't take long for him to catch me. I made several turns, but he stayed right with me. Where was a cop when you needed one? I couldn't get away from him. We were going very fast.

I came to an intersection. The light was red, but I ran the light trying to attract a police officer. It looked clear, but just before I made it all the way through the intersection, an SUV clipped my back end sending me spinning until I hit a pole. My head hit the windshield and I was knocked unconscious.

When the police and paramedics arrived, Jimmy was nowhere to be found. The police were waiting to question me at the hospital. I was unconscious for about three hours. When I woke up, Tony was sitting next to me, holding my hand and crying.

"Hey." I stroked the top of his hand with my fingers.

"Denise. Oh baby. I've been so worried about you. I thought I was going to lose you too." Tony rambled.

I smiled at him. "What happened?"

"You were in a car accident. The police found you in your pajamas with no shoes. What were you doing out like that?"

I remembered trying to get away from Jimmy, but not the accident. I told him and the police the whole story. Jimmy was arrested on assault charges. I was released from the hospital three days later. Tony spent all of his free time taking care of me and nursing me back to health. I got a letter from Jimmy apologizing for everything. He wished me happiness with my new man. I never heard from him again. I moved in with Tony and we have been very happy. We are planning to be married next spring.

It's been great having my own doctor that makes house calls.

THE END

STOLEN MOMENTS

The persistent ringing of the phone jarred me out of a sound sleep. Bobby stirred next to me but didn't awake.

"Hello, this better not be a prank," I said into the phone, still half asleep.

"Allison, are you awake?" I heard the voice of my boss, Joe Brown, of Brown, Wiskoff, and Jones Advertising Agency, ask.

"No. I'm sleeping like all normal people do at this hour."

"Jump into the shower. I need an enormous favor."

"Come on, Joe. It's five am, Saturday morning."

"It's important, Ally."

"So is my sleep."

"Roy Colby of Halpern Stores, Inc. has an appointment with Tom to discuss the possibility of signing on with us. I don't have to tell you what his business could mean to our firm."

"That's all very nice, but couldn't you have waited to tell me this wonderful news at a more human hour…say some time after noon?"

"That's not the reason I called. You've got to pick him up at the Bangor Airport. His flight to New York was cancelled at the last minute."

"Why, me?"

"Because you're a pilot."

"That's just a hobby, not what you hired me for."

"Please, Ally. If it weren't so important I'd never ask."

"Oh, stop groveling. I'm up already…."

"I knew I could count on you."

"Never again. Especially this early in the morning. Promise."

"I promise. Now get going."

Not wanting to wake my fiancé, I left a note on his night table explaining where I'd gone. I told him I'd be back late afternoon.

I drove to the airport where my plane was ready, having called ahead. It was a two-seater prop. To most people it looked like a large remote-control model toy. To me it was a roundtrip ticket to heaven. I loved flying and have had my pilot's license since I turned eighteen. Flying gave me a feeling of exhilaration akin to nothing else.

I found the flight to Maine refreshing. The few cobwebs of sleepiness that had lingered during the ride to JFK had been blown away. I was wide awake and enjoying the beautiful sky.

I landed at Bangor and proceeded to the accommodations counter to page Roy Colby. Having never seen him before, I expected an older man, not the youthful one that approached me.

He was tall and athletic looking. His hair was short and as black as night. He had eyes that reminded me of warm cocoa. In short, he was simply gorgeous. I hoped that neither my facial expression nor my accelerated heart-beat gave away my thoughts. All he carried was a leather attaché case and an overnight bag.

"Are you the pilot?" he asked, sounding skeptical.

I nodded. I couldn't blame him. First of all, most people expect a man, not a woman. And secondly, I looked quite young. Hardly anyone took me for twenty-five wearing makeup. Now, I stood before him with my hair tied up in a ponytail and not a drop of makeup on my face.

He seemed lost in thought for a moment. Perhaps he had cold feet and didn't want to chance flying with me, but that wasn't the case for he finally said, "Let's get rolling, then."

I smiled and led the way out to the plane. There wasn't a long wait to take off because the air traffic was still light. I expected him to make a comment about the size of the plane. He didn't. Perhaps he was used to taking puddle-jumpers. Better for me.

We gained altitude. The visibility was good. I could see him admiring the beauty that the sky offered. He didn't seem to be much of a talker. I didn't mind that at all because I'd rather concentrate on the flight.

We were leaving the Maine airspace and entering New Hampshire when we hit a pocket of turbulence. In a small plane like ours it always felt like an amusement park ride when the plane bucked. Many people got airsick. I stole a quick look at him to see if he was affected. Luckily he didn't seem to be. I was relieved. I hated it when people got sick on the plane.

The even hum of the engine was interrupted by a sputtering noise. The sound immediately sent shivers down my spine. The instrument needles began to flutter. Something was terribly wrong. Then I noticed the needle on the oil gauge had dropped considerably.

I contacted the control tower of the nearest airport. I had to land quickly.

"We're going to crash, aren't we?"

"Not if I can help it," I said, motioning him to be quiet.

"Yes, my coordinates are...oh, dear God..."Brace yourself, Roy!" I commanded as we began to rapidly lose altitude. There was no time to make it to an airport. We had to make an emergency landing.

"Look for a small clearing!"

It was almost useless. All we could see were miles of endless trees.

"There!" Roy shouted over the noise and the loud beating of my heart.

"I see it! Pray!"

91

I headed towards the clearing, fighting with the steering and desperately needing a miracle. The noise was deafening. I saw my whole life pass before me. I thought of Bobby. It looked like we were on a collision course with a thousand trees. I saw snow. Then everything went black.

When I finally regained consciousness, Roy was standing over me. I had no idea where I was. The last thing I remembered was heading for the clearing. There was a look of concern on his face along with some cuts and bruises.

"Good, you're awake," he said smiling. "How do you feel?"

I touched my throbbing head. "I...don't know. Alive." I tried to get up, but collapsed as everything began to spin around me.

"Here let me help you," he said as he gently lifted me up. "You probably have a concussion. There's a beauty of a bruise on your forehead."

Being so physically close to him sent shock waves through my body. I knew it was wrong to feel that way, being engaged, but I couldn't help it. As he carried me away I caught sight of the plane. The heap of twisted wreckage looked more like an accordion than a plane. We both were lucky to be alive.

I felt bruised but knew everything was still intact. From what I could tell, Roy seemed to have received only a few minor bruises and scratches. Yes, we were very lucky, indeed.

"Did you radio for help?" I asked.

"The radio was damaged in the crash and is inoperable."

"Damn!"

Roy looked worried. I wanted to reassure him and I guess, myself, when I said, "Don't worry. There's probably a search party looking for us now."

"Only if it doesn't snow," he said. "Look at the sky."

He was right. It did look like snow--and lots of it. We were stuck in this place in the middle of nowhere alone together.

Roy had carried me to a small shack he had found nearby. He must have scouted out the area while I was unconscious. Inside the shack were few amenities, but it was better than nothing, especially with a snowstorm on the way.

Roy had set me down on a small rickety cot. From where I was I could see a few cans of soup and beans stacked on a shelf over the small sink, not much more in the way of food. If we weren't found soon, we'd starve to death.

Roy went outside to gather wood to build a fire. It was getting colder. The temperature had dropped about fifteen degrees and neither one of us had more than the jackets we wore.

I felt the cold dearly for every bone in my body ached. But along with the ache from bruises was another kind. One I didn't want to have. I should be thinking of Bobby. Yet, I found myself drawn to the tall dark, handsome man with whom I was stranded. Thinking of him, I fell asleep.

I opened my eyes. There was a fire going.

"Are you feeling better?" Roy asked.

"Yes."

"Would you like something to eat?"

I nodded. We ate some beans and spent the rest of the evening talking. He told me about his business and how he got started. He had been a poor boy that got lucky. Unfortunately, he wasn't lucky enough to keep his marriage together and told me about his ex wife. There was a new woman in his life, but he was wary of marriage.

Roy asked about me and I told him about Bobby and my career. What I thought was boring, he found interesting, so I talked away.

The snow began to come down hard. It was upsetting to know that a search party wouldn't be out looking for us until it stopped. The eerie howling of the wind didn't have much of a soothing effect on me, either.

There was only one small cot in the shack. Roy and I would have to share the single cot if we wanted to survive the night. We needed our collective body heat to keep warm. He was very careful not to injure me on the side that was bruised, but the closeness drove me crazy. Snuggled together, I couldn't help but notice he felt something, too. I had this terrible desire to reach out to him. I chastised myself for it. I had never cheated on Bobby, nor had I ever considered being with another man before. Yet, here I was so damn tempted…I prayed I didn't moan in my sleep. What helped me fight the temptation was the fact that my body ached and needed rest. Sleep must have come quickly, because the next thing I knew, it was morning.

When the snow abated Roy went out for more wood. If the visibility remained clear a search party would surely come looking for us.

There wasn't much for us to do. Roy rummaged through the shack and found an old beat-up pack of cards with all 52 cards intact. We played every card game we knew. We ate sparingly of the little food we had. But most of all, we talked. Normally I would have found all this boring. I didn't with Roy. I enjoyed every moment with him. He was the most interesting, and, oh God, the most desirable man I had ever met. I was falling in love with him.

Feeling extremely guilty, I tried to fight the growing feelings I had for Roy .Yet, the more I fought, the stronger they became. I knew it was all so terribly wrong. I had a wonderful, caring fiancé at home who was probably going out of his mind with worry. The guilt was overwhelming, yet, Bobby was at home and here I was many miles away with a gorgeous, exciting man. I hoped we were found soon before I weakened and gave in to my desire. I was finding it harder and harder to resist. The man who was once a stranger had bared his soul to me and was no longer one. I wanted this man more than anything. If it hadn't been for Bobby....

I tried to concentrate on Bobby. I closed my eyes and attempted to visualize his face. I couldn't. My God, how could I not picture the face I saw every day? The guilt began to consume me.

Then reality hit me. What if we weren't found? What if it began to snow again? What if we ran out of food? We could die out here. Should my last days be filled with guilt and unfulfilled desire? Or should I die satisfied in the arms of a desirable man?

"Allison, what's wrong? Are you in pain?" he asked, pulling me towards him on the cot.

I shook my head. Not physical pain, I thought, as my desired rose.

His eyes met mine. They said what I wanted to hear. It was getting harder to breathe as my body began to anticipate what was to follow. He took my face in his strong hands and gently kissed me. I kissed him back longingly. Our kisses became fiercer and deeper as our tongues dueled for possession. He slid his hand under my blouse, found a breast and cupped it. The mere touch of his hand on my skin left it burning. I let my hand drop and rubbed his hardness. A moan escaped from his lips. Within moments our clothes were on the floor.

The fire crackled and glowed as we made love, franticly, as if there'd be

no tomorrow. Perhaps he had come to the same conclusions as I had. Or maybe he desired me as much as I had wanted him.

His unbridled passion rose to meet mine. I had never felt this way before, not even with Bobby. I doubted if I'd ever feel the same again. We had reached our sweet releases almost simultaneously.

Now that the urgency was over, we began to make love again, more leisurely this time. As I lay back on the cot, Roy began to cover every inch of my body with butterfly kisses and nearly drove me out of my mind. The desire in my eyes and my audible moans told him I was more than ready to have him inside. He filled me with his hardness and within moments, I climaxed again.

Lying together in the afterglow of our lovemaking, I tried to memorize his beautiful face and sensual lips, as well as the touch of his hands on my body, savoring every moment. I knew we had begun something we could never finish. If we were rescued, he would return to the woman waiting for him and I would go home to Bobby. But as Roy reached for me once again, I knew I couldn't stop myself anymore than I could control the weather.

94

We awoke to the noise of a rescue helicopter. Roy and I were both realists. We knew we'd never be able to see each other again. As much as I wanted to, I knew I couldn't. I was still engaged to a wonderful guy and I wasn't ready to trash my life with Bobby based on one night. Last night would remain a beautiful fantasy and its sweet memory would last forever.

When we parted, I kissed Roy goodbye and wished him happiness. He bid me the same. As I struggled to hold back the tears welling in my eyes, I thought I detected a slight misting of his beautiful dark eyes. Perhaps he'll never forget our beautiful night together, either. When he walked away, he would be taking a part of me that no one could ever replace.

I tried to pick up the pieces of my life where I had left them. Even though I tried to make the wonderful night I had spent with Roy Colby a memory, I couldn't. When Bobby made love to me, I imagined it was Roy. The more I tried to forget Roy, the more he became a part of my dreams.

Bobby and I began to disagree over everything. Little things he did began to irritate me. I started to get on his nerves. Perhaps his unhappiness fed off of mine. I blamed myself, for I feared I was the one who had changed. Bobby realized our love was slipping away and tried to recapture what we had. After dinner one night, he took out two airline tickets.

"What we need is a vacation," he said, "so we can jumpstart our relationship. We've let it become stale."

I truly wanted to recapture the feelings I once had for Bobby. I was willing to try anything. "Perhaps you're right. Where are we going?"

"How's does a week in Jamaica sound?"

"Great. I'll ask for vacation time the first thing Monday morning."

The persistent ringing of the phone waked me up. I glanced at the clock. It was seven o'clock. I reached for the phone nearly dropping it on the floor.

"Ally, I'm sorry to wake you up, but it's important," Joe Brown, my boss, said.

"Nothing is more important than my sleep. Remember?"

"This is. You must pick up a very important client at the Teterboro Airport."

"Hey, didn't you promise me something?"

"Yes, but I'm sure that you'll have a favor to ask of me some time."

I was ready to blast him when I remembered that I needed vacation time.

"Okay, who is it this time?"

"Alan Jones. And he specifically asked for you."

"I've never heard of him. How did he get my name?"

"You can ask him when you pick him up. Have a nice safe trip."

"Yeah, thanks, Joe, you're all heart."

"I know, bye."

I had Alan Jones paged at the accommodations desk. I smiled as I remembered the first time I had Roy Colby paged.

"Allison..." A familiar voice interrupted my thoughts. Suddenly I found it difficult to breathe. My heart began to beat so hard against my chest it threatened to come right through. I turned. Roy Colby was standing there. I blinked a couple of times to make sure it was really him. I began to walk towards him. Then suddenly I was running. Roy scooped me up in his strong arms and our lips met. The desire I had tried so hard to deny spread quickly to every nerve ending in my body. Breathlessly, we unlocked each other to speak.

"I wasn't sure you'd come had I used my real name. I went home and tried to resume my life, but I couldn't. I knew you had someone else, but I had to see you again."

"Oh, Roy. Things haven't been too perfect between Bobby and me, either. I tried to forget you and that magnificent night we shared. But, every time I closed my eyes, it was you I saw, not Bobby. I'm afraid...I'm in love with you."

"That's what I came here to hear. I want to spend the rest of my life with you—that is, if you'll have me."

"Darling, if that's a proposal, here's my answer." I threw my arms around him and gave him a passionate kiss.

THE END

TORN BETWEEN
TWO LOVERS

I was very blessed at thirty-eight years of age. I had a successful career as a court reporter, making lots of money, and working at the Daily Center, downtown on Randolph Street, right in the heart of the loop area. But I also had the most wonderful man in the universe in my life, Thomas Porter.

My Thomas was a very tall black man, over six feet tall, with a beautiful chocolate complexion, and gorgeous black hair. He was a male model, and I was the lucky woman who captivated his essence.

Thomas and I met when he came to the Daily Center for a legal matter he was involved in, suing his modeling agency for misrepresenting him. Of course, Thomas won the settlement and moved onto another modeling agency. His career was still booming at forty years of age. Thomas had the physical presence and definite aura about himself, which attracted modeling agents. He was right now still in demand. I was truly proud of my man. We had been dating for a year, and the relationship was still going strong.

Of course, the downside of the relationship was the fact that Thomas did most of his modeling in New York, so I missed him like crazy. But we ran up the telephone lines, and when I wasn't slated to work, I'd visit him there. Right now he was in New York for a week on a photo shoot for a popular magazine, so I still missed him, but I knew he was making lots of money, and doing the one thing he loved best.

When everything was going great in my personal life I had to meet a Cuba Gooding Jr. look-alike, by the name of Skeleton. He worked in the same building so we met in the cafeteria. Skeleton was gorgeous with his weird name, but for some reason I was very attracted to him. I knew it was because Thomas was spending so much time traveling, that I was just lonely. It was the only explanation. Skeleton was an attorney so we had a lot of conversation going. I was threading on dangerous territory, but that didn't stop me at all.

Thomas and I met every day for lunch, and our conversations were easy on the ears. I felt so guilty. It was like cheating on Thomas, but Skeleton was a very fascinating man.

Besides, I had been waiting for Thomas to propose to me for months, and if he didn't take the bait then I was going to rethink my relationship with him. We had been dating a year, and it was time. When he returned home, I was going to bring up the subject. I needed to know where I stood with Thomas. We loved each other, so marriage was the next avenue on our agenda.

I truly enjoyed my lunches with Skeleton. He had seven sisters, and the antics that went on his house was hilarious, especially their names. I knew his name was funny, but Cinderella, Beauty, Little, Mappy, Kitchen, Jamaica, and Flower were his sister's name. I laughed so hard I was literally weeping. His mother was definitely from another planet.

"My mother's name is Book."

I almost lost it as I hysterically wept this time. I had never laughed so much in my life. Thomas was a serious kind of man, so it was very difficult getting a laugh out of him, so Skeleton was a different distraction to say the least. I loved laughter because it took away some of the pain.

Skeleton and I continued our lunches, and I found myself looking forward to them, disappointed that it was a Friday, and I wouldn't see him again until Monday. Of course he wanted to go to a movie on Saturday, but Thomas would be back in town, and I had to talk serious business with him. I was also anxious to see Thomas. Did I need two men in my life? I was beginning to doubt my own handle on reality. One man was always enough for me, and I loved Thomas, but Skeleton was becoming very important in my life.

Later as I opened the door for Thomas, I smiled. He could still bring out the bubblies in me as I embraced him. "Hi. I missed you."

"Not as much as I missed you, baby, but right now I need a shower and then some tender loving care. I'm exhausted."

"Then take your shower, and I'll be waiting for you."

"Sounds like a plan to me."

I watched him stroll into the bathroom as I walked back into the living room and sat down. Thomas spent a lot of time in my apartment so we were practically living together since he had a key, and I had one to his apartment in Beverly. He had clothes in the closet, and toiletries in my bathroom, so living together was the operative word.

I tried focusing on Thomas, but thinking about Skeleton and his mother's name, not to mention his seven sisters, got me laughing to myself. How did he survive such a madhouse? Skeleton was becoming more interesting every day. How would it feel making love to such a man?

"What's so funny?"

I jumped at the sight of Thomas' naked body. He didn't like clothes, and if there weren't a law preventing you from going out naked, then Thomas would be there in full force. Thomas was a bag of chocolate slim fast bars and more. Staring at his throbbing member, I knew he was all hot and ready for me, and I felt the same way, glad that my body could still moisten at the sight of him. I wanted him. Something was happening to me because I was probably in love with two men.

I shook my head and focused on Thomas.

He had the same idea as he walked toward me with that 'I want to make love to you' look on his face. I smiled as I stood up, removing my attire and ready for action as my naked body gleaned with anticipation of what was next.

Thomas took both of my hands and passionately kissed them, and then he tilted my head, and fastened himself on my lips. I closed my eyes as my body began doing flip-flops as our kiss intensified with our tongue meeting. I still had it hot for Thomas, who teased me with his lips and tongue, bringing me to an immediate boiling point of rage, but of a sexual frustration. I wanted him like I had never wanted anyone. Thomas could still exercise my pleasure, and I was grateful to know this fact.

Thomas and I loved kissing, and we could literally kiss for hours, of course, which was impossible, but our kisses lasted more than the lovemaking process. When we finally released our lips, our eyes met because we were both swollen in sweat.

The next minute, Thomas grabbed me and carried me to the bed where he attacked me with his lips, kissing and teasing my breasts until my nipples couldn't stand his actions much longer. I let the flames take over my body as I screamed out my pleasures. He left my breasts and then covered my neck with kisses, and the entrance to my breasts again as he ate me like I was whipped cream, or an ice cream cone, licking to the essence of my core.

My flame was burning out of control, and I wanted him inside of me like a mouse wanted cheese. "Take me," I cried.

I heard his grunt, knowing that was his signal for more joy to come. Thomas took his own sweet time making love to me. He had the patience of a saint, which was why he could stand in one pose for hours, and modeling was the only career for him. I didn't have that much as my loins ached with the need for him.

When Thomas was finally heating up his own body, he added protection and gently entered me as I screamed out his name, feeling the sparks of a chemical imbalance shoot through my body. I was a thunderstorm raging outside, distracting the rain for the moment, but letting its anger show.

Thomas was crying out his satisfaction as he pumped for dear life, the bed rocking back and forth. Thomas, of course was a big man so the bed couldn't stand his weight most of the time as I let the pleasure entice my soul. When we were finally spent, our lips met again, and we kissed for ten minutes, feeling our bodies light up like a match to a cigarette. Thomas entered me again and we finished the uproar of pleasure that we just couldn't get enough of.

I felt so good and I didn't want the feelings to stop. Thomas and I blended well together, and I was a nut for even considering dating another man. I didn't need anyone else because Thomas was all the man I needed. I knew he was faithful to me, as our lips met again, and our tongues mated. He was definitely the man for me. I had to let Skeleton know that I wasn't available on Monday. I couldn't destroy the relationship I had with Thomas. It wasn't worth it.

After we ate and Thomas got some much-needed rest, we watched a movie, but I wasn't into it as Thomas was. I needed to talk. "Honey, can we talk seriously about something?"

"Okay."

"When are you going to propose to me?"

I stared at the look of shock on his face. "Did I utter the wrong words?"

"It's only been a year, Belinda. Why the rush? You and I are practically living together so why rock the boat? Making it legal will cause a lot of unwanted problems. I love you and there's no other woman for me. I just don't have the time."

I didn't like his words. "So if you weren't such a busy model, you'd be playing the field," I snapped. "How dare you?"

"Honey, let's not argue. This movie is good. Let's snuggle up and enjoy the rest of the evening. Next week I'll be in Paris. Would you like to come with me?"

I wanted to jump at the chance, but I remembered Skeleton, and the fact that Thomas wanted his cake and eat it too. "I can't get off," I lied.

"Are you sure?"

"Maybe another time. I want to get married Thomas. I'm almost forty and I'm not wasting another year."

"Let's not give ultimatums because they don't sit well with me."

"I'm just letting you know that I'm not about to spend five years of my life with you, and then someone else enters the picture, and I'm left out in the cold. I need security."

"Whatever."

He focused back on the television as I fought the rage inside of me. Who did he think he was? There were definitely other fish in the sea. I couldn't wait until I saw Skeleton.

It was soon two weeks later. Thomas was spending time in Paris, so I was enjoying my time with Skeleton. We had been going out every night to the movies, and dinner, and I loved it. Skeleton was funny and I loved his sense of humor. Besides, he was open to the security of marriage. It was nothing for Thomas and everything for Skeleton.

I was sitting outside of his building, staring at his condo. I knew if I went inside the two of us were going to make love. Did I have the nerve? Could I make it work? I didn't want to compare the two men because Skeleton was his own unique individual self. Was I ready to make love to another man? Would I call out Thomas' name? This was all new to me. I had never dated two men at the same time.

I stared at the building not finding the urge to get out of the var. Skeleton told the security guard that I was expected, so all I had to do was show my identification and head up to the 20th floor. Why did I have butterflies in my stomach? You'd think I was a virgin or something.

I was nervous, and I did feel guilty. Thomas was in Paris working his ass off, and I was sleeping around. Or was he just working? How did I really know? I headed for the building.

Skeleton and I sipped delicious red wine. We had been talking for an hour when his gaze became more than just a normal gaze. He wanted me because I could see the lust in his eyes, and I wanted him, having fought my sexual feelings for an hour. I put my glass down on his unique coffee table, loving the feel of his condo as I met his eyes. I was giving him the signal that I was ready and I wanted him.

Skeleton didn't need a second wind as he stood up and took my hand. I followed him to his bedroom, where we exercised the lust inside. When he touched my breasts, the heat lit up my body and I knew it was on now. I closed my eyes and let the magic take over.

An hour later we laid spent, and I was wondering why Skeleton didn't kiss me. Thomas and I couldn't get enough of each other's mouths, and lips. As I laid in his arms, I wondered, and had to know. "Why didn't we kiss Skeleton?"

"I don't like it because of the germs."

I was stunned beyond words. "Excuse me?"

"It's not necessary. Our bodies are meshing together and that's enough in my opinion of germs. I'm going to take a shower and cleanse my body. I don't like to be smelly and digested with germs for long."

I couldn't believe him as he walked into the bathroom, shutting the door. What gall he had? All men had faults, and Skeleton had a deep one. I hysterically laughed. Two men in my life were the greatest.

When Skeleton walked back into the room he was wearing his shorts. "Now it's your turn, and then we can snuggle together. I can't lay with you until your body is clean."

I laughed again. "Of course. I can spend the night."

"I was hoping so. We're going to become engaged very soon, Belinda. You're the kind of woman I want to spend the duration of my life with. We understand each other, and the sex is great. What do you think?"

I nodded my head as I walked into the bathroom. Words failed me, but if Skeleton proposed before Thomas, then may the better man win. But was it so easy? I was still in love with Thomas.

At work the next day, I was taking a break when I noticed Thomas. What was he doing here? I thought he had a photo shoot today. "Hi. Let's go over here and talk." This was too dangerous. I didn't want to run into Skeleton.

"I thought you'd be surprised to see me," Thomas said. "I changed the time of the photo shoot because I wanted to give you something. Will you marry me? I don't know when, but I'm not going to lose you. I love you."

I couldn't believe it as I stared at the gold diamond ring. I was muted to the spot.

"Hello," Thomas shouted.

"I will marry you," I cried.

Thomas smiled and put on the ring. I was now engaged to the man I really wanted to marry. I let the tears fall and then it dawned on me that Skeleton could walk in any moment. I had to get Thomas out of here. "Let's go out to celebrate, honey. I have some free time."

"Are you sure?"

"I'm positive."

"I have to get back, so another time. I just wanted to show you that I love you."

"I'll walk you out." I hurried him to the elevator hoping Skeleton didn't get off. We were safe as the doors opened and we hurried out of the building. I was so glad to reach Thomas' car. "I love you," I cried.

"Me too," he cried.

Walking back into the building and out of the elevator I ran smack into Skeleton. I hurriedly hid my ring. "Hi."

"I have something for you."

I knew it had to be a ring. "Can we meet after work, Skeleton? I have to see the judge on an urgent matter." I hurried down the hall knowing he was staring at me. Again, what in the hell was I going to do?

I went through the motions of working, but I kept staring at my ring, and thinking about the one that Skeleton would present to me. Could I avoid him all together? Who did I want to spend the duration of my life with? I couldn't accept two marriage proposals? I had to end it with one of them before they found out. Who would be the one?

I took the scared way out, and left early, faking a headache, and hurrying home from work. I turned off the ringer on my telephone and made sure the doors were locked. I knew I'd be meeting Thomas at his place, so there was no chance of Skeleton barging in. I sat in my living room, in the dark, contemplating my next move. Skeleton would be angry with me but I needed to evaluate the situation. I managed to get myself involved with two men. I loved Thomas, but I was falling in love with Skeleton; they both were good in the sack, but Skeleton didn't like kissing. Thomas and I had a lot of things in common, but Skeleton and I shared a lot of things also. I was definitely torn between two lovers. It was the wee hours of the morning when I fell asleep.

The constant knocking on the door brought me awake as I surveyed the room. I was in my living room, and someone was banging on my door. I wiped the sleep out of my eyes and hurried to it. "Hi Thomas. What time is it?"

"Eight o'clock in the morning. I've been calling you all night. Are you okay?"

"I overslept. Come in and let me call the office. Where is your key?"

"I left the house in a haste and forgot it. Is everything okay with you?"

"Just fine. I'm the happiest woman in the world."

"And I'm the happiest man. Who is Skeleton?"

I almost fainted. "Someone from work."

"He was standing at your door when I made my presence known. I told him that my fiancé was unavailable, and he was very surprised to know that you're engaged."

I felt like dying on the spot. "Skeleton is too bossy for my taste. He's an attorney."

"He was so devastated."

"He liked me, but I told him that I was taken, and now he has the proof. I'm going to take a shower."

"Let me run it for you."

I smiled. "Thanks." Thomas hurried into the bathroom, and I let the tears fall. Skeleton found out about Thomas, and now I wasn't torn between two lovers any longer. Thomas was the man I'd be spending the duration of my life with. How would I face Skeleton at work? I frowned as I walked into the bathroom to be with Thomas. The matter was definitely solved for me, but why did I feel so lost?

THE END

I'M ADDICTED TO SEX

My next-door neighbor, Desmond, was totally hot. To me he was nothing less than a bronze god, but he didn't even know I existed. Why should he? I was a skinny kid with pigtails. I followed him around whenever I could. He was my Prince Charming whom I intended to marry one day despite the obstacles.

One day he had a girl in his room. The shades hadn't been pulled down all the way so I was able to peek in. They were both naked and doing it. As I watched, I pretended that I was the girl, memorizing the entire act.

By the time I had grown into a woman, Desmond was gone. Some say he was forced to leave after having gotten somebody's wife pregnant. Other said it was because he had gotten a girl pregnant and wouldn't marry her. I didn't believe any of it. After all, he was my knight in shining armor. No matter what, I never truly let my vision of Desmond go. It lingered in the back of my mind waiting to surface. After all, dreams do come true. One day he'd be mine.

I worked for a moving company scheduling jobs. That's how I met James. He's wasn't much of a talker, nor a hot guy. He was really nice, though and dependable. Whenever he came to pick up his pay check he'd hang around and talk for a few minutes. I began to look forward to our little chats. One day things seemed different.

"Hi, James. I have your paycheck right here."

"Thanks. Um, Shawna, there's something I'd like to ask you."

Before another word was said, the phone rang. I excused myself and took the call.

"Sorry. Now what were you saying?"

The phone rang again. I made an exasperated face and he laughed. I took the information down and made the appointment.

"Tell me quickly before the phone rings again."

"I have two tickets to a basketball game. Would you like to go?"

I liked basketball and said yes. He seemed happy and we made a date. I found out that the quiet, sort of shy guy had a great deal going for him.

We had a quick dinner before the game and I learned more about James. He was one of five boys, always having to defend what was his. That included his last girlfriend who ended up marrying his older brother.

"Wow! That must have been real tough getting over."

He shrugged. "I lived. It just wasn't meant to be."

I marveled at his attitude wondering how long it really took to feel that way. I was certain that it must have truly hurt. He quickly changed the subject to a happier one and before long we were on our way to the sports arena.

The game turned out to be excitingly close and we both ended up with sore throats. It was late when we arrived back at my door, so James gave me a quick good night kiss. It was a sweet kiss, nothing earth shattering. Before he left, though, we made another date for Saturday night.

I liked James. I knew it wasn't fair to compare him to Desmond, but I did. The memory of Desmond would always be with me and no man I ever met seemed to measure up to him. Of course, deep down inside I never stopped believing that Desmond would be mine some day.

James didn't seem to rush into anything, especially relationships. After what he experienced, I could understand why. We had been dating for several weeks and saw each other often at work. One could only describe us as close friends until the velvet night we crossed the line and became lovers.

James had taken me to a movie. We came back to my place for coffee. Usually we'd kick off our shoes and have a lively discussion of the movie over coffee. But, from the moment we entered my apartment things were different.

"I don't really feel like coffee tonight, Shawna. How about a beer?"

"Sure, just a sec."

I came back and handed him a beer and sat down next to him with my own. We began to talk about the movie when suddenly James stopped talking in mid sentence. I looked into his warm brown eyes and saw something I hadn't noticed before. My eyes answered his and a moment later we were in one another's arms kissing. The kiss was deep and passionate, no longer platonic.

We continued to kiss until we were both breathless. James' hands explored my body over my clothing. The desire to rip off my things became stronger by the passing second. His hardness pressing against my thigh told me that he felt the same. The sofa was far too small for what we had in mind so we kissed our way into my bedroom.

James was a gentle and considerate lover. He slowly worked his way down my body using his tongue and hands to bring me to a feverish pitch. With all this mind-blowing foreplay, it didn't take long for me to climax. He must have held himself back waiting for me to be pleasured first, for as soon as I had finished he came.

"You're beautiful, Shawna," he said and kissed my nose.

I smiled and kissed his lips.

We cuddled together and enjoyed the afterglow until sleep peacefully came to us both.

A few days later I forced myself to go to the supermarket. I hated to go supermarket shopping and had given new meaning to bare cupboards. And for more emphasis, I threw in an empty refrigerator as well.

Like a scene from a movie, I was coming around one aisle when like a ghost from years past, Desmond Washington and his sister, Jasmine were coming towards me. I recognized them both instantly. The shock must have shown on my face for Jasmine asked, "Do I know you?"

I smiled and said, "I'm Shawna Reid—"

"Little Shawna Reid?"

"I'm not little any more."

"Man oh man, can I see that."

"How are you two?" I asked.

"We're both fine," she replied, continuing to appraise me. "And you?"

"On my own, since my parents moved."

"Well, you sure look like you can take care of yourself," Desmond added.

I looked at him. He had become even more handsome. I could feel every sensory cell in my body come alive just by being so close to him. As for Jasmine, I wondered if she was the same snotty person I remembered. She used to treat me so badly and hated to see me come around. My mama used to say, "That girl will make some man miserable one day."

"What brings the both of you back here?"

"Our Aunt Jane passed away. The funeral was yesterday."

"Sorry to hear that. Was she sick?"

"She suffered for years with cancer. I'm glad God finally took her."

"How long will you be staying?"

"Probably till the end of the week," she responded at the same time Desmond said, "It depends."

She gave him a look. I nearly broke out in a giggle. So that answered my question. She hadn't changed.

"Des, dear, we must be going."

Desmond nodded and turned back to me. Then he asked the magic words I always longed to hear. "Would you have dinner with me tonight?"

Of course I said yes as I watched Jasmine's face fall. There would be words spoken on that ride back to wherever they were headed. I practically skipped around the store after that encounter. Shopping would never be the same for me.

106

Driving home the magic began to fade as reality freshened my memory and brought me back to my senses. What about James?

I had totally forgotten about James as if he never existed in my life. We had a beautiful relationship and yet I suddenly felt as if it never happened. Well, what was I supposed to feel? After all, the man I had loved and adored all my life had just asked me to dinner. I had dreamed and made love to him in those reveries a thousand times. Now it was all in my grasp. I could hardly believe it was actually happening.

I won't deny I care for James. He's a wonderful guy, dependable and caring. But he's not gorgeous and exciting like Desmond. I reasoned that there was no commitment between James and me. Had we been engaged, that might have made things a little more difficult. I decided to let my heart lead the way. I was totally blinded by my desire for Desmond.

Desmond picked me up and took me to a cozy little restaurant. He had given me a single, long-stemmed rose that I had put in a vase. But between the compliments on how I looked and his admiring glances, I felt like the most beautiful woman in the world. And being with him, the luckiest, as well.

We shared a bottle of wine with dinner, but I hardly needed alcohol to make me high. Sitting so close to Desmond was intoxicating enough. I still had trouble believing that it wasn't a dream.

Afterwards we stopped into a lounge to dance. I had some more wine, but being held so close to Desmond in his strong arms literally put me over the edge. Visions of him making love to that girl years ago flashed before my eyes.

One dance later, Desmond nuzzled my neck and whispered, "Let's go somewhere where we can be alone."

I knew exactly what he meant and nodded. I had made love to him so many times in my dreams that I felt I knew what it would be like. Within minutes we were walking into a motel room.

"I can't believe how beautiful you've become, Shawna," Desmond said before covering my mouth with his. The kiss was overwhelming. As he began to caress my back, I became that girl in his bed.

He began to remove my clothing, one article at a time, kissing and teasing me at the same time. I was so wet with desire that I began to pull him closer.

"You want me baby, don't you?" he murmured in my ear as he began to caress my breast.

My response came in the form of a moan. His knowing how much I wanted him, didn't speed his actions up. Instead he purposely took his time slowly skimming his lips over every inch of my body driving me nearly out of my mind. I cried out in the midst of such agonizing pleasure, "Desmond, please!"

He seemed to ignore me and continued his kisses further down my body. He flicked his tongue in and out of my navel turning it into an erogenous battlefield. Nibbling at my inner thighs, I knew he had brought me to the brink. I could wait no longer and pulled him up towards me. He poised a moment over me before he lowered his lips to mine. Finally, at that moment, he entered me. Filling me completely, it wasn't long before we both reached our climaxes.

"That was beautiful, baby," Desmond said before he promptly rolled over and began to snore.

It felt like a letdown. There was no sweet afterglow talk or cuddling—nothing. I guess he was really tired from the stress of all the traveling and the funeral. I figured I'd let him sleep a while. When it seemed that he wasn't going to wake I called a taxi and left.

Desmond called me at work the following day and apologized for falling asleep.

"I'm sorry about last night, Shawna."

"Don't be."

"But I should have never fallen asleep like that—I mean—what you must have thought of me."

"Look, it's been a long stressful week for you. I understand."

"I should have taken you home."

"It's okay, Desmond. I forgive you."

"Enough to see me tonight?"

"Yes."

"Great! I'll pick you up at the same time."

James walked into the office. He wore a concerned look. I had barely given him any thought during the last twenty-four hours.

"I had left a message on your answering machine."

"Sorry, but I hadn't noticed."

"Where were you last night?"

"Out with a friend."

"All night?"

"What is this, twenty questions?"

"Why are you jumping down my throat? I was worried about you, that's all."

"Well, you don't have to since I'm a big girl and can take care of myself."

"You don't have to be nasty about it."

"Who's being nasty?"

The phone rang and interrupted us. When I looked up again James was gone. With Desmond occupying my mind 24/7, I merely shrugged off the disagreement with James.

That night was nearly a repeat of the night before. Instead of having a leisurely dinner Desmond seemed to want to rush through it

108

and have dessert, which was me. Suddenly I felt as if I meant nothing more than an easy lay for him.

"What's the matter, baby?" Desmond asked.

"When will I see you again?"

"I dunno, baby."

"You really don't intend to see me again, do you?"

He turned away and said nothing. I felt miserable. It was obvious that I had created a dream that really didn't fit the man. He gave new meaning to 'beauty is only skin deep'.

I went home and cried myself to sleep. I had sent the only real man in my life packing. With the pain that he had experienced in his past, our relationship was as good as over. I had thrown it away. And for what? I felt like a total fool.

The next day I called in sick and didn't bother to get out of bed. I was feeling sorry for myself and praying for a miracle that would turn back time to before Desmond showed up.

Coming out of the bathroom, I heard the doorbell. Looking like a disaster, I had no intention of answering the door. Whoever was out there was persistent. Finally I heard, "Shawna, I know you're there. Open the door!" It was James!

Why did he come? He sounded angry. Was it to give me back the things I had left at his place? It didn't matter. Seeing him would make me more miserable.

"Go away!"

"Not until you talk to me."

If he continued to make a racket someone was going to call the police. I let him in to get it over with. He looked miserable.

"Before you say anything," he began, "I have something I want to say to you."

Here goes, I thought...

"I lost one woman because I didn't fight back. I don't intend to lose another. I love you and want you---"

"But---"

"Let me finish—"

"There is no other man! I love you---only you."

"You do? Forget what I was saying. Come here," he demanded as he reached for me.

I went into his arms seeking the true warmth of his embrace. Tears of happiness intermingled with those of relief and streamed down my face. I had nearly lost this wonderful man and wouldn't be so reckless with his love again. From now on, my dreams would be of him.

THE END

SEX PLAY
He Used Me Then Dumped Me

I turned my head and met his gaze. I could hardly bear the closeness another moment. I wanted him. And I knew that he wanted the same thing I did: To make love.

I licked my bottom lip as I longed to touch my lips to his. No longer able to resist the urge, I slowly moved closer. I breathed in his scent of cedar as I kissed his waiting lips.

Savoring the kiss, he ran his hand along my shoulder to the back of my neck and up into my braids. Blood pulsed through me at a rapid rate. Heat coiled in my abdomen. I was on fire. Lifting me to the top of his desk, the urge for him to take me right then and there overwhelmed me.

Sliding his hands down the side of my breasts, he let his thumbs caress my nipples, bringing them to rigid peaks. The way he clung to me made me feel somehow whole again. Like a part of me had been missing for a very long time. And now he had replaced it.

I could feel my heart racing and the desire building inside me.

Taking hold of my shirt, he unbuttoned it and slid it off my shoulders. His mouth journeyed to my neck, kissing it tenderly. I wanted him like I'd never wanted anyone in my life; loved him as I'd never loved before.

Paul Michael Barrett was the embodiment of my dreams.

Bringing my arms down from his neck, I helped him slip his shirt over his head. He buried his fingers in my hair and loosened the tie, letting my braids fall to my shoulders.

I could feel Paul's heart pounding beneath my palm. I wanted to tell him that I was falling in love with him, but knew he wasn't ready to hear those words. At least this afternoon, I could show him.

Slowly, he undressed me as I did the same to him.

"You are so beautiful," he whispered.

I brought my hand to his cheek and gently stroked it. Pulling me closer to him, he covered my mouth with his. Slowly, he moved his mouth across my cheeks, down the front of my neck and to my shoulder.

Paul guided me back on his desk. Lying beside me, he teased me with his fingers by running them up and down my bare stomach. He brought his mouth back to my swollen lips and my mind reeled from desire.

Cupping a breast in his hand, he brought his mouth to my nipple.

110

Like a fire, his lips burned over the soft mound. His tongue outlined the small circles of my nipples until the hardening peaks gave proof to my own desire.

A throbbing sensation overtook my body as his hand slowly moved over my flat stomach and dallied between my legs. While his fingers drove me mad, he teased my nipples with his tongue.

I looked at him and saw such passion in his eyes, the heady feeling of knowing that he desired me as much as I did him, consumed me. Today, he would make love to me for the first time. I wanted it to be slow and hot. I opened my legs to him readily.

Consumed by his warmth, I gripped his back as he slowly, gently entered me.

The phone jangled wrenching me from my daydream.

"You ruined the most beautiful dream."

"Let me guess, it was about Paul. Listen, Girlfriend, I don't see how you can love a man who's a virtual recluse," Shandaliz scolded through the phone lines.

I moved the phone receiver to my other ear and whispered, "I never said I loved him. Besides, I know what's on the inside. He's a sweet charming man. A true-blue philanthropist. His voice is so rich, so oh, I don't know, it gives me chills."

"But he hides from the world."

"The accident left him scared. True, plastic surgery repaired the physical scars, but it takes time to heal the emotional ones. I know I can help him. He needs me." As I turned in my chair the outer door to the office opened. In my haste to look busy, I knocked over my pen and pencil cup. The writing utensils scattered across my desk and rolled onto the floor.

A woman peeked her head around my door and said, "Is Paul in?"

"Hold on please," I said then pressed the button on the telephone. Turning my attention to the beautiful woman who had just entered my office, I said, "I haven't seen Mr. Barrett yet this morning. Sometimes he comes in through his private entrance. Let me check."

I pressed the intercom. "Mr. Barrett are you in? You have a visitor."

"Yes, I'm here Kenisha. Who is it?"

The woman smiled and said, "Just tell him its Lisa."

My chest burned at the sensuous tone she used. If eyes could change color, mine would be green with jealousy.

I pressed the button, "She said her name is Lisa."

A chuckling came over the speaker then, "Send her in."

I motioned to his door. Once she entered I picked up the telephone and groaned."

"Shandaliz, this beautiful woman just stopped by to see Paul and he chuckled when I announced her! I think he's finally seeing someone—and it's not me!"

"Get real Kenisha. It's been three years!" Shandaliz's voice boomed so loud I had to pull the phone away from my ear. "If he wanted you he would have made a move by now. Girlfriend, you have got to move on!"

I absorbed what my friend had said as I picked up the pens and pencils and placed them back in the cup. I felt sorry for Shandaliz. She was good at dishing out advice on affairs of the heart, but I didn't believe Shandaliz had ever really been in love.

"Kenisha, are you still there? Or have you hung up on me?"

Shuffling papers on my desk so Shandaliz would think I was busy doing something, I replied, "I'm still here, but I have work to do."

"Okay. But at least think about what I said."

I heard the click of the disconnection and replaced the receiver back in its cradle. Almost everyone in the Real Estate office had taken the day off. Most people used the day after Thanksgiving to create a long weekend. I liked working in the peace and quiet, though. As the office manger for the large business, it was difficult to keep up with all the paperwork. I relished days like this when the office was empty and I could catch up on things.

I had hoped Paul would have the same idea so I could spend a little alone time with Paul Michael Barrett—the man I loved. Now he was in his office with a beautiful woman probably doing things that I've dreamed we would do together. Images rushed through my mind as I imagined his hands caressing the most intimate parts of my body. His touch, his scent, his rich, deep voice. Just the thought set me on fire again. Then my image was replaced with Lisa's and the backs of my eyes burned with tears.

I stared at the oil portrait of Paul painted just a month before the plane crash. His deep brown eyes appeared to be staring down at me. There was a dimple in his left cheek, and a cleft in his chin. And I wanted to run my fingers down every inch of his chest, touch every hair, and feel every ripple of muscle.

Since the plane crash, he had become a virtual recluse. Paul sustained burns over seventy-five percent of his body. After multiple surgeries all his physical scars were healed, but the emotional ones were still there.

Paul's best friend was aboard the small Cessna 172 with him when the plane crashed. He was the sole survivor. Monique, his fiancée, was supposed to be on the plane too. Luckily for her, they had had a huge fight and she refused to get on the plane.

After the crash, she dumped Paul. She even went as far as to move to another state.

The abandonment by Monique had devastated Paul. He totally withdrew from human companionship and became a recluse.

Since the accident, he hired several additional real estate agents. They do the legwork and meet with the clients face-to-face. Paul remains the Broker of the agency, but he rarely sees anyone. Yet he manages to close almost every deal.

I'm one of the few people that has had contact with Paul—but I don't have much. The only time I see him is if he needs me to bring him a file or some business related item. But what I long to do is to touch him, to breathe in his intoxicating scent, to have his sensuous lips touch mine and for him to touch me and flame the fires I can't extinguish on my own.

Now for the first time since the crash, a beautiful woman has stopped by to visit with Paul. I was happy he'd finally been able to break free of his shell—but I had wanted it to be with me.

"Kenisha, Kenisha are you there?" Paul's voice echoed through the intercom, startling me back to reality. I jumped and knocked over the pen and pencil cup again.

After gathering the last pen and placing it back in the cup, I took in a deep breath to try to hide my disappointment and then pressed the intercom switch answering, "Yes, Paul. What can I do for you?"

"I was beginning to think you stepped out."

"No, I'm here. I'm the only one crazy enough to come in after Thanksgiving."

"Kenisha, you're my most dedicated employee—you're not crazy."

Only dedicated to being near you, I thought to myself. Paul asked for a file. I retrieved it and headed toward his office. I swiped at my damp cheeks before opening the door, and then straightened my suit. We were alone today and I had wanted to take advantage of the situation—and him. I had wanted him to take me on his huge mahogany desk. I had wanted to be the one to bring him back to the world of the living.

But Lisa had beaten me to it.

When I entered his office it was empty. I heard him yell from his private restroom, "Just put it on my desk."

My heart sank at the realization that he was probably in there with that woman! I tossed the file on the desk and went back to my work area.

Tears stung the backs of my eyes as I sank into my chair. My dream of the two of us getting together was just that—a dream. I should have listened to Shandaliz. Paul was a hopeless case. I was a fool to think I was the one that could save him.

The intercom came to life again. "Kenisha, can you get me 1999's Multiple Listing Book?"

"Sure, I answered."

My heart sank at him treating me just like an employee, even if that was what I was. I wanted to be so much more to him.

I went to the bookcase looking for the book he requested. It was a large compilation of all the real estate that sold in the area during 1999. Finally I saw it on the top shelf—way over my head. Even in heels I was only five foot two inches. I rolled a chair into position, climbed onto it and reached for the book. It was stuck and I tugged and jerked at it. Finally it came free.

But the jerking motion caused the chair to roll and I lost my balance. I screamed as I fell off of the chair. My arms outstretched to break my fall, they took the brunt of my weight and then my head grazed the legs of the desk.

Paul's alarmed voice came over the intercom. "Kenisha... Kenisha! Are you all right?"

I lay there, assessing my injuries. It didn't take long, I hurt all over. A warm wetness dripped down the side of my face. When I tried to reach up to feel my head, I let out a scream of pain.

"Kenisha. If this is a game, it's not funny. Answer me!"

"Paul," I answered. "Paul, I'm hurt."

For some reason he couldn't hear me.

"Kenisha, I'm not falling for this. Answer me!"

The pain in my shoulders, head and wrists throbbed with every heartbeat. My hands had broken my fall all right, broken being the operative word.

"Paul," I cried. "Paul, please help me."

I heard his office door open. Since I was laying face down on the floor, when he neared me, I could only see his black loafers.

"Oh, God! Kenisha, don't move. I'll call for help."

I heard him on the telephone calling for an ambulance. When he returned to my side, his reassuring hands stroked my head.

When he spoke to me again, his voice was tender, almost a whisper. "You'll be okay, Kenisha. I'll make sure of it."

My dreams of being close to Paul, of him touching me had finally come true. I relished each second before I lost consciousness.

The medical team poked, prodded, examined and performed every test known to modern medicine at Paul's insistence. I had a slight concussion, a broken collarbone, a broken right wrist and my pride was shattered.

But Paul Michael Barrett had touched me.

He'd spoken sweet, reassuring words to me.

The doctor came by to talk with me. Because of my concussion and loss of consciousness, his instructions included that I wasn't to be alone for at least twenty-four hours. Before I could say anything, he also told me that Mr. Barrett was having a car take me to his home.

In my mind, this last bit of information made the fall almost worth it. Paul had arranged for me to stay with him. Could all my dreams come true after all? What would Lisa think?

When I arrived at his place, I was amazed at the size of his estate. I knew that Paul was financially set, but I had had no idea he was this wealthy.

I longed to see him, to be close to him. When he rescued me, he put my needs before his own. That was something he hadn't done since the accident. He'd been so wrapped up in his own pain that for a time other peoples' feelings came after his own needs. Oh, he was still a philanthropist. He still had charities he donated to. He was still a generous boss. But he didn't allow himself to become active in other's lives.

Now he had. He was taking an active part in my life—in my recovery.

I whispered aloud, "That unselfish act, could it be? Is it possible Paul really cares for me? Could he be in love with me, too?" I knew I was letting my imagination run amuck, but I couldn't help it. I'd been in love with Paul for so long him returning my love was all I could hope for.

Once the car stopped in front of the house, a woman took care of seeing me into Paul's home. I looked for him, searched for him, but he wasn't around.

I wanted him to take care of me, but that wasn't to be. His maid tried to take care of my every need, but there were some things that only Paul would be able to fulfill.

"He must be with Lisa," I mumbled.

When night fell, the maid tucked me in. It was the maid who made sure I wasn't in need of anything and then she left me—alone.

I didn't even know her, but I hated Lisa.

The medication the doctor had given me for pain made me drowsy and I slept through the night.

I dreamed of Paul.

When I awoke in the morning, I was instantly aware that I wasn't alone. A hand rested on my wrist. I could see remnants of burn scars covering the hand and reaching up and under the sleeve, and I knew it was Paul's hand. His head rested on the edge of my bed.

Paul's head!

I longed to stroke his jet-black hair, but my free hand was in a cast. An ache to be in his arms, for him to kiss me, overwhelmed me as I watched him sleep. He began to stir and he sat up with a start.

Paul turned and looked at me. I looked into his dark brown eyes. I pulled my hand from his and touched his cheek, letting my fingers linger. When I finally spoke, my voice quivered, "Thank you for rescuing me."

To my surprise, Paul didn't pull away. Instead, he brought his hand to mine. He carefully held it in his, and then slowly returned both to the bed. His brows drew together in an agonized expression. He whispered, "You scared me yesterday."

"If I had known this would be the result, I would have scared you a long time ago." Embarrassed, I lowered my gaze to where his hand held mine and then continued. "In case you haven't noticed, Paul, your office manger has fallen in love with you.

Squeezing my hand a little tighter, he said, "I noticed. I just didn't dare believe it." His expression stilled and grew serious. "I couldn't take a chance that you would love me and leave me like Monique."

My heart pounded with excitement and butterflies fluttered in my stomach. I was delighted and nervous at the same time. And I wasn't about to waste the one opportunity I had to get Paul to trust me. "I would never treat you like Monique. She was a fool. Either she didn't know she walked away from the best catch in the world or she's just an idiot."

Paul shifted uncomfortably in the chair, and his eyebrows rose. "Maybe you just don't know the real me and once you do you will leave, too."

"I've known the real you for many years. What made you take a chance on letting me get close to you?"

"Actually, I didn't plan this. I came in last night to make sure Jean had taken care of you. I sat down to watch you sleep, and I must have dozed off."

Sitting up in the bed, a smile formed at the corners of my mouth. "I'm glad you did."

He kept himself deceptively composed. "When I awoke, I could see it was light and sensed you were awake. I knew it was too late to sneak out." Shrugging his shoulders in resignation, he said, "So I made a decision to throw caution to the wind. I've thought about this for so long, I figured it was time to take action."

"You've thought about letting me get close to you?"

"I've wanted to let you into my life for so long, but I didn't want to scare you away. I sit in my office and daydream about you all day long. You're so beautiful and I'm—" his voice faded.

"You're a gorgeous hunk. Don't you realize that the beauty you have inside shines through your eyes? You're a wonderful man and nothing can hide that. You just need to let yourself get past the accident. Yes you look a little different. But you are still you. I can help you if you let me in. I won't run out on you like Monique."

"I've never given anyone a chance since she dumped me."

I wondered about Lisa, but was afraid to say anything. Afraid of what his answer would be. Instead I said, "Oh, Paul, didn't you ever once believe you could trust me?"

116

A melancholy frown flitted across his features and he shook his head decisively. "No. Never."

I searched his eyes and could still see a little fear, a touch of pain. In a soft reassuring voice I said, "I love you for who you are. I believe if you love someone you love everything about them, the good and the bad."

Paul got up from the chair, sat beside me on the edge of the bed and brushed a tendril of hair out of my eyes. "I'm amazed at the way you have never treated me any different since the accident. Everyone else does."

Amused, I smiled as I cocked my head to the side and asked, "I've always believed in you, Paul. Always."

Placing his hands on my shoulders in a possessive gesture, he said, "I see that now." The pressure of his hands on my shoulders lessened as he brought a hand to my cheek and caressed it as he asked, "What on Earth made you believe in me even when I didn't believe in myself?"

I arched my left eyebrow. "Love."

Paul leaned toward me, his eyes brimming with tenderness and passion as he cupped my chin tenderly in his warm hand. "You definitely have my attention."

He pressed his lips to mine, caressing my mouth. It was a kiss that spoke what words alone could never say. I melted to his touch. It was what I had dreamed of for so many years I wondered if it was all just another daydream. He was gentle in his fondling as he unbuttoned my gown. His scent smelled of cedar and pine and all man.

I wrapped my arms around his neck and buried my nose in the fabric of his shirt. This was real.

His fingers found my nipples and they immediately responded to his touch. They were firm, erect, and aching for his mouth to cover them. As if he could read my mind he took my breast in his mouth and every sense in my body awoke. I tingled from head to toe and I didn't want any of these feelings to ever end.

I pushed his shirt off his shoulders and discovered that most of his burns had healed well on his chest and upper arms. I kissed his bare skin. It tasted salty but gave me a sweet thrill.

"Girl, I've never wanted anyone as bad as I want you."

"I want you, too, Paul. There are too many clothes separating us."

"You're right."

In seconds nothing kept his body from mine. We lay together on the bed. He trailed kisses along one side of my throat and then the other. His fingers wandered down my belly until it found the nest between my legs.

I thought I would go mad if he didn't touch me immediately. His kisses continued down my chest, on each breast and then down my abdomen, past my belly button. Then he dallied just at my hairline.

I dug the tips of my fingers into his shoulder. My cast was heavy and in the way but I wasn't going to let it put a damper on the moment.

"Paul, don't tease me any longer. You're driving me mad."

He looked up into my face and smiled. "That's my plan, baby. To drive you absolutely mad with passion."

He kissed the top of one thigh and then the other. And then finally he found my pleasure spot and I fell off the precipice of sanity.

I writhed and wriggled and tried to get away. I had never experienced so much pleasure all at once. I didn't think I could stand it another minute. "Oh, Paul, I want you inside me now, now. Oh, please, now."

He didn't hesitate. In an instant he'd thrust deep inside me and we were connected as one. We moved together and all was right with the world.

"Sweet girl, I love you. I've loved you from a far for so long this all seems so surreal. Please tell me you're truly here with me now."

"I'm here, Paul, and I'm all yours. Don't ever let me go."

Our rhythm quickened but our timing was in unison. Our souls had finally found their mate and I knew I was finally home. In an instant we both climaxed and I was sure the bed moved beneath us—or was it the Earth?

Afterward we lay in each other's arms. I was so overcome with emotion it was all I could do to keep the tears at bay. How many times had I dreamed of this moment? And now we were finally together.

But I wondered what now? What about Lisa? Where did she fit in? Was he seeing both of us, or was he really all mine?

Two weeks passed and most of my bumps and bruises were healing well. Paul insisted I stay with him for my entire recovery, and there was no way I was going to refuse him. I knew in my heart that I belonged by his side—that together we could both be better people; that we could be who we were supposed to be in this world.

Paul had no problem letting me get to know the real him, he wasn't hiding from me any longer. But I felt like he was hiding me. He insisted we keep our relationship quiet and I couldn't help but wonder if it was because of Lisa.

When he came home from the office, I had an entire night of entertainment and romance planned for the two of us. A quiet dinner on the patio, filled with candlelight, and then a night of dancing at the Silver Lady Jazz Club downtown.

I knew the dinner would go smoothly, but I wasn't sure how he would react to the Jazz Club. I hoped and prayed he would be willing to give it a try. It was past time that he let the world know that we were together. And if he thought I was going to let him see Lisa and me at the same time, he was in for a rude awakening.

"How's my beautiful lady tonight," he said as he kissed me on the cheek?

"I'm doing fine. I have a very special evening planned for us tonight. Why don't you shower and change and meet me on the deck."

"Be back in a jiffy, Babycakes."

Fifteen minutes later he sat across from me at the table. The midnight blue tablecloth was the perfect setting for the white china place settings. Candlelight danced across the crystal wineglasses and set my heart aflame with desire.

Just being in his presence made me hot for him. But tonight couldn't end like every other night had for the last two weeks—in bed making mad, passionate love. It was time he let the world know we were together. So far our love affair had been this big secret. I was tired of feeling like the other woman. I wanted everyone to know that I was his and he's mine—all mine! There was no way I was going to share him with Lisa!

After dinner I tried to ease the idea into the conversation.

"You still like jazz, Paul?"

"Very much."

I smiled. "Good. I have the perfect evening planned for us tonight."

"What do you mean?" his voice had an edge of nervousness to it.

"I made reservations at the Silver Lady for us."

"Kenisha, no."

"Now, Paul, listen. I've reserved a quiet table for us in the corner of the club. It's time, Paul. It's time to let your friends know I'm in your life. I don't like being hidden like I'm some dirty little secret."

His jaw rocked from side to side. He was quiet a long time; so long it scared me. I wondered if I had pushed too hard, too fast.

Finally he spoke. "I thought you accepted me for who I am."

"I do, Paul. Now it's time for you to accept me for who I am. I'm a person who has feelings. I don't deserve to be treated this way."

"What are you talking about?"

"You have character and values. You have compassion and love. You have a soul that touches mine in a way no other human being could ever come close to. But I don't understand why you are keeping me a secret from your friends, my friends, and our co-workers. Please, Paul, I deserve better. You don't have to jump in feet first. We can take it slow, but you have to start sometime."

He cleared his throat. "I don't know if I can."

"Why? Are you ashamed of me? Or are you more in love with Lisa than I am. I won't share you, Paul"

He looked puzzled. "Baby, God, no. I'm not ashamed of you and Lisa is my cousin. I'm afraid of being humiliated again if you leave me."

"Lisa is your cousin? Really? You're not dating her?"

"No! I'm finding a new house for her and her husband. I haven't dated anyone since Monique left me. She humiliated me. She left me when I needed her the most. I felt like I must be some terrible person if she could leave me while I was still in the hospital."

"Oh, Paul. You're not the heel, she is. And I'm not Monique. I would never do that. Don't you know how much I love you?"

He took in a deep breath. "Yes, I think I do. I'll go if you save all your dances for me."

I was out of my chair and in his lap in two seconds flat. I hugged him and kissed him. "I'm so proud of you. Welcome back to the living."

We went to the Silver Lady that night and danced until closing. That was the first step in a long line of little steps. But it wasn't long before Paul announced to the world that we were engaged.

We've been married two years now and I didn't think there was any way our life could get any better. That is until the stick turned blue.

Tonight I'm going to tell Paul that our family will be getting a little larger—we'll be bringing another Barrett into the world.

THE END